THE SUMMER CAMP SWAP

SUMMER FLING
BOOK 3

KAIT NOLAN

TAKE THE LEAP PUBLISHING

1

"I need you to impersonate me."

From the faded corduroy sofa in her tiny, studio apartment, Sarah Meadows rolled her eyes, though her sister on the other end of the phone couldn't see. "Did you forget to renew your driver's license again? Because it expired back in January."

"I wish it were something that simple," Taryn said. "I've got a serious problem."

Sarah tensed at the words. "What is it this time?" She tried to keep the judgment out of her voice. Really, she did. But it was hard. So much of her twin's adult life had been a train wreck, and it seemed Sarah was routinely the one called upon to pick up the pieces and deal with the fallout.

"Well, you know I was supposed to be done with this private tour guide gig day after tomorrow and flying back East in time to start the new job at Camp Firefly Falls on Saturday, right?"

"Yeah. You've got orientation starting this weekend."

"I'm not going to make it back in time."

Oh, not good. Not good at all. "Why? What happened? Did your flight get cancelled? Because it's not too late to reschedule."

"No. This job came in last night—a two-week-long trek for some Hollywood muckitymuck."

Sarah couldn't stop the exasperated sigh. "You are *not* blowing off the camp job for one last guide trip." Dear God, she'd thought her sister was past this kind of impulsivity.

"No, it's not like that. I told Danny I couldn't do it. But he's threatening not to give me my last month's pay if I don't stick around and do it."

"You haven't been paid in a *month?*"

"Room and board were covered, and I figured if I didn't have the money in hand, I couldn't blow it on anything stupid. Except now I risk not getting paid at all, and I need that money, Sarah."

That was putting things mildly. Three years before, Taryn's unfortunate taste in men had re-sulted in a short relationship with one Jax

Howorth—not his real name—who'd taken every dime of Taryn's money, trashed her credit, and left her under a mountain of debt. She'd been slowly, painstakingly climbing out of that hole ever since.

Sarah sighed. "How much are we talking?"

Her sister named a figure that had Sarah's mouth dropping open.

"You're getting paid that much as a guide?" Maybe she'd chosen the wrong career. Not that anybody became a grad student to make money. The hope was that you'd make enough when you finished the degree that you'd pay off whatever student loans you'd acquired before retirement.

"Rich people will pay for all kinds of things. And this producer guy, or whoever, is willing to give me a five *thousand* dollar bonus to stick around."

That had all of Sarah's alarm bells ringing. "Are you sure he doesn't expect you to do something more than be a trail guide?"

"Positive. He's flamingly gay."

Well, that was something, at least. "So, what exactly are you asking?"

"I want you to go to Camp Firefly Falls and be me for orientation. I'll be done with this job, get paid, and be back in time for the certification test. Nobody will be any the wiser."

Sarah shoved to her feet and began to pace. Ten steps to the kitchen. Fifteen to the window overlooking the busy Brooklyn street. Five to her bedroom door, then start again. "Taryn, this isn't like fooling our high school teachers. This is a job! One that you're qualified for, and I'm not. And what about you actually learning the stuff you're being certified *for*?"

"I've learned the handbook backwards and forwards, and there's nothing a camp in the Berkshires can throw at me that's harder than what I've been doing in Wyoming."

"That may be, but *I'm* not trained for any of this! How do you expect anybody to believe that I'm you?"

"It's not that complicated, sis. You're in good shape. You're a trained lifeguard, a runner. And God knows, you haven't met a subject you can't study up on and pass a test for. You just have to spend a couple weeks learning their policies and procedures, helping get camp set up, readying cabins, and that kind of thing. Easy peasy."

"Yeah, that's what you said when you convinced me to fill in at cheerleading practice so you could meet up with that college guy. 'Kick high, shake your thing, you'll be fine,' you said, 'they'll never know the difference.' Only you failed to mention the pyramid, and trust me, when it all came down, everyone knew the difference." Sarah felt a twinge in her back at the memory.

The noise at the other end of the line sounded suspiciously like a stifled snort of laughter. Taryn cleared her throat. "In my defense, I didn't think they would try the pyramid. Man they were pissed." This was always the way. Her twin saw the humor in everything and never seemed to manage to take anything seriously.

"Not making your case here, Sis."

"But pissed at me, they were pissed at me. And no human pyramid at camp, no polyester, and no shaking your thing unless you're so inclined. But preferably not, because, you know, I have to work with these people."

"I'm smarter than I was at seventeen. Too smart to let you drag me into this. Besides, I do have a life. Responsibilities. I can't just pick up and go play you for two weeks."

"Oh, come on. Like you can't take a couple weeks off from your thesis?"

Sarah fought not to grind her teeth. "I can't, actually. I'm on a very strict schedule in order to finish in time to defend in August and start the doctoral program in the fall." She'd scrimped and saved in order to take the summer off from any assistantships so she could just write and be done with the thing. She wasn't about to waste that time.

"But just imagine how much clearer your head will be after getting out of the city. You said yourself, you have a hard time writing there. You've been dying to get out of New York. This is your chance to recharge a little. And it's beautiful. You could take your camera, finally have some of the nature you actually *like* shooting pictures of."

A car horn blared from the street below and somebody shouted an inventive curse in... was that Portuguese?

A muscle by Sarah's eye began to twitch. "By working for you."

"Pleeeeeeease," Taryn wheedled. "Think about it, Sarah! Five *thousand*. It's enough to put a serious dent in the stupid debt. Enough I might be able to pay the last of it off by the end of the summer, so I can finally have a clean slate."

A clean slate. That had been Taryn's Holy Grail since Jax had walked out of her life. He'd been her wakeup call, the last in a long line of poor decisions. The school of hard knocks had taught her what no one else could, and she was finally ready to grow up. If she finally could get free of the mess Jax had created, she'd be able to do that. And

Sarah would be able to stop worrying about her and focus on her own work.

Maybe.

But could she really afford two whole weeks away?

The living room wall rattled as something solid slammed against it from the apartment next door. A moan and the rhythmic thumping that followed told her it was the newlyweds going at it again, instead of a nice, helpful home invasion that would put an end to the ear-splitting noise violations they engaged in multiple times a day. The eye-twitch ramped up to a full on headache. Not only were they supremely distracting, but their enthusiastic amour only served to highlight exactly how long it had been since there'd been a man in her life.

Not that she was looking.

Sarah pinched the bridge of her nose. "You *swear* this is something I can pull off?"

"Absolutely!" Taryn assured her.

She was probably going to regret this. But maybe her twin was right and getting back to nature would help break the writer's block that had been plaguing her for months. At the very least, maybe she'd get some shots to replace the artwork on her walls.

"Okay. Against my better judgment, I'm in. Tell me what I need to do."

"GOOD MORNING, STAFFERS!"

From one of the picnic tables set up down by Lake Waawaatesi, Beckett Hayes watched his new boss, Heather Tully, address the assembled crowd. Oh yeah. His buddy, Michael, had done well when he'd married her. The cheerful blonde looked absolutely in her element. And why shouldn't she? Camp Firefly Falls—summer camp resort for grown-ups—was her brain child, and it had been a roaring success.

"It's going to be a super busy couple of weeks as we finish prepping for our first session of the summer—Singles Week—so we'll be throwing you all into the deep end with that one."

"Deep end is right," the guy next to him whispered. "I was here for that last year. It's like policing a damned orgy."

"Great," Beckett drawled. He'd dealt with some of that in his last job as national park ranger. Herding drunk, horny people was never fun. It almost always ended in insults and often with beer or other questionable liquids spilled on his uniform.

"Now, some of you will be here all summer and some will be in and out, depending on the specifics of the session, but everybody has to pass their camp certification by the end of next week to keep our insurance company happy. That said, we want all of you to have fun yourselves. Here at Camp Firefly Falls, we work hard and play hard. The work begins bright and early at eight every morning. You can pick up your daily assignments at breakfast. We wrap in time for dinner at six, with evening activities planned so you can get to know your fellow staff members."

The collective staff cheered.

"This afternoon, we're getting started with a swim test."

"Are you serious?" someone called from down front.

"Camp rules. Everybody has to tread water for two minutes, then swim out to the raft and back. Anybody who does not pass will *not* be on any water activities for the summer. Anybody who's not already suited up, go change. We get rolling in fifteen minutes!"

Beckett held himself back from the minor stampede toward the staff cabins to change clothes. He was already set with board shorts and a T-shirt. While waiting, he scanned the remaining faces, noting the animated conversations and laughter. A lot of these people were returning staff, and a fair chunk had been campers here before the Tullys bought it and turned it into a resort, back when Camp Firefly Falls had been a regular sleep-away camp for kids.

Beckett hadn't been one of them.

Michael wandered over and plunked down on the other side of the table. "Settling in okay?"

"Getting there."

"Cabin working out for you?"

Beckett laughed. "It's like a damned penthouse suite compared to some of the places I lived with the park service. Listen, I want to thank you again for giving me a job this summer. After the—" He cut himself off, not wanting to get into the mess of his former position. "Well, my prospects weren't great. This is really saving my ass." The summer's work would buy him time to figure out his next move.

"Hey, it's our gain and my pleasure. They were wrong for firing you."

Beckett jerked his shoulders. "Yeah, well, I was far from the only one." His position and those of many other had been cut along with funding for so many of the national park programs. Things were improving some with the new administration, but those kinds of reversals took time to actually trickle down.

They both looked out over Lake Waawaatesi, glistening in the afternoon sun. It was gorgeous, soothing, and a far cry from the Ivy League campus where they'd met.

"Never would have thought we'd end up here when we were busting our humps for our MBAs," Beckett observed.

"Maybe not me, but you walked away from the crazy a lot sooner than I did."

In his last year of grad school, Beckett had walked out. Of the classroom. Of the MBA program. Away from Dartmouth. He'd never looked back. "Wasn't gonna make me happy."

"I wish I'd figured the same out sooner. That whole corporate culture nearly cost me my wife."

"But it didn't," Beckett observed. "This place brought you two back together."

Michael sighed in obvious contentment. "Seems fitting since we were camp sweethearts as kids."

He tipped back his water. "You're a lucky bastard."

"Yes, yes I am. And hey, who knows? Maybe you'll meet your match this summer."

Beckett cocked an eyebrow at his friend. "Come on, now. I expect that kind of crap from Heather. Not from you."

Michael just grinned. "We've got a bulletin board up in Pinecone Lodge with pictures of all the couples who've gotten together here. It's filling up."

"You, sir, are full of shit."

Laughing, Michael shoved back from the table. "Just don't let Heather hear you say that. She'll try to matchmake you."

"I do not need the complication of a woman in my life." His own prospects were so uncertain at the moment, why would any woman even consider getting involved with him? He'd had few enough girlfriends over the years. None of them had been able to tolerate the semi-itinerant lifestyle of a park ranger. When his transfer to Yosemite had come up, his girlfriend at the time hadn't wanted to move with him, and he hadn't cared enough to want to stay. Since then, Beckett hadn't bothered with anything more than casual. If that had gotten old some time ago, well, such was life right now. He had other things to figure out.

"They're the only complication that's worth it." Michael's voice pulled Beckett back to the present.

"Spoken like the happily married man you are. And on that saccharine note, I believe I'll take my position at the starting line." He stripped off his T-shirt and toed off his Chacos, leaving them in a neat pile on the picnic table as he went to join the thickening crowd on the dock.

He found himself next to a long, lean woman bent in a forward fold. He made a valiant effort not to stare at her ass in the snug, racer-back swimsuit and ended up admiring her gorgeously toned legs instead.

"See something you like?" The wry tone had him yanking his eyes away like a teenage boy caught peeping in the girls' locker room.

Busted.

"Sorry," Beckett muttered, gaze now firmly on the raft anchored out in the center of the lake. "You just look—" Was there any way to finish that sentence that didn't make him come off like a perv? "—like you know what you're doing."

"I should. I've been swimming competitively practically since birth." She straightened. "I'm Taryn."

He interpreted the proffered hand as a sign of forgiveness and turned to take it. His own name died on his tongue as he found himself faced with the biggest doe eyes he'd ever seen.

Well hello, Bambi.

"Hi."

A corner of Taryn's mouth quirked as she gave his hand a perfunctory shake. "May the best swimmer win."

"Win wha—"

The scream of an air horn signaled the start of the test. Taryn dove for the water, as did everyone around Beckett before he could get his brain in gear. She'd already surfaced by the time he dove in. The chill lake water was a shock to his system, clearing the haze of lust from his brain.

"Two minutes!" Heather shouted. "Starting... now!"

His feet and arms automatically began to tread, keeping him afloat. A few feet away, Taryn was already facing the raft, her dark blonde hair slicked back like a seal.

"In a hurry?" he asked.

She glanced over her shoulder one corner of her mouth quirked. "Eye on the target."

"You know this isn't a contest, right?"

Her lips bowed into a full-on grin that sucker punched him more than the icy lake. "Everything's a competition."

Beckett had done everything in his power to get away from competition in his life. But something about that smile pulled at him and invited him to join in the fun. He had a feeling competition with Taryn would be anything but the senseless, boring grind he'd walked away from. So he readied muscles honed as a boy in the surf off Myrtle Beach, and when Heather blew the air horn again, he went for it.

He made it to the head of the pack in four strokes, but Taryn was faster. Her freestyle was a thing of beauty, slicing cleanly through the water as if she'd been born to it. Beckett dug deep, pulling his focus back to his own form. Half a dozen strokes and he'd closed the gap to two lengths. Ahead, Taryn slapped the raft and dove, popping back up and heading toward shore. Beckett tagged the raft himself and switched to butterfly for the return leg. He caught up with her at the halfway point. Seeing what he was about, she shifted smoothly into a butterfly stroke herself, and they both raced for the finish line.

Taryn beat him by two strokes. Beckett could hear her crow of victory as she slapped the dock.

"You are a freaking mermaid," he gasped.

She slicked her hair back and beamed. "Yes, I am. God, that felt good!"

A shadow fell over the two of them. Michael. "You realize we have no prizes, right?"

"Maybe you should," Beckett suggested. "Because that was damned impressive."

"Maybe we'll just move things around so she's on lifeguard duty instead of paired up with you for rock climbing."

"Looks like tomorrow we get to go to *my* playground." Beckett grinned, turning to the mermaid. Something had wiped the smile clear off her face. In fact, she looked a little sick. What was that about?

He hauled himself out of the water and reached down to offer a hand to Taryn. "You okay?"

Eschewing his hand, she hoisted herself cleanly up, the water sluicing off that long, lean body. "I'm fine." She reached for a towel, hastily wrapping it around herself before muttering, "See you tomorrow."

Then she was gone and Beckett was left wondering what the hell he'd done wrong.

Michael smirked at him. "What was that you said about not needing the complication of a woman?"

"Still true. But I'm breathing, so I can appreciate the distraction of one when she appears."

His buddy just laughed. "I call that denial, but whatever helps you sleep at night, pal."

2

The lodge was buzzing with conversation when Sarah stumbled in at 7:15 the next morning. She didn't make eye contact with anyone, didn't talk. Her entire attention was focused on finding the coffee. As long as she got some in the next two minutes, no one would get maimed, and she'd probably manage to maintain her cover.

"Good morning."

Sarah held in a whimper. How dare anyone expect her to converse before caffeine? Homicide on her mind, she turned to find a mug held out to her.

"Oh, thank Jesus." She snatched it from the big, masculine hand, and took a hefty swallow, not caring that the coffee scalded her mouth. The heat from the mug soaked through her hands, taming the beast and melting away her habitual foul greeting of the day.

Lifting her gaze, she found her competition from the swim test yesterday. He was grinning at her, clearly amused. Sarah didn't even care. He'd brought her coffee. As far as she was concerned, that was a life debt. "You, my friend, have just performed an act of the greatest public service. No one will die today."

"Glad to hear it. Since there was no official prize for winning yesterday, I figured not having to fix your first official cup of camp coffee would have to do."

"Better than any trophy. Come to me, my sweet, sweet nectar of the gods." She took another sip, slower this time, and rolled it around in her mouth, savoring with a contented sigh. It was excellent coffee—rich and bold and black as midnight.

He laughed. "Not a morning person, I take it."

"Not even a little bit."

As the fog of sleep began to lift, Sarah took a moment to study her benefactor. He looked annoyingly bright-eyed, a Camp Firefly Falls T-shirt stretched across the broad shoulders that she now knew could execute a perfect butterfly. That was almost sexier than the sculpted chest she could still picture with rivulets of water running down to the board shorts that hung, dripping, low on his lean hips.

And why are you cataloging his finer features? You won't be here to enjoy them after the next couple of weeks.

Perhaps her man-drought was taking its toll, but there was no harm in admiring the view. He'd done the same to her on the dock. And hadn't that been a nice boost to her ego? After all the time sitting on her ass in classrooms and labs or camped out in study carrels, she still had something worth admiring. She lifted her gaze to his face. Not classically handsome or the vaguely geek-chic she'd become accustomed to in academia, but his was an appealing face. All sharp angles, with a week-plus of dark scruff shading that square jaw that was icing on a very delicious package. He'd be next to the picture of *rugged* in the dictionary. Who knew that worked for her?

Sarah lifted the mug. "And to whom do I owe this beneficence? I didn't catch your name yesterday."

"Beckett Hayes. And you're Taryn the Mermaid. Fitting."

Sadly, for the next two weeks, yes.

Since he'd brought her coffee, she graced him with a smile. "Meadows. Taryn Meadows. Nice to meet you." Taking another sip, Sarah glanced around. "You seem to know the lay of the land. Where are our schedules?"

"Right this way." Beckett led her across the room to a table set up at the tail end of the buffet.

The schedules had been alphabetized by last name. Sarah found hers and skimmed it.

"According to Heather, the staff has been split into four groups for orientation." As Beckett continued to talk, Sarah skimmed the list. "We'll all be rotating through the assorted classes—first aid, CPR—"

"Bartending? Really?"

"So I'm told." He shrugged. "Anyway, between all that, we'll be doing overall prep of the facilities and checking equipment."

That didn't sound so bad. When Michael Tully had mentioned she'd been assigned to rock climbing, she'd nearly panicked. But Taryn was entirely qualified to deal with that, and she'd be here to take her rightful place by the time it really mattered. Sarah had eyes in her head. Surely she could look at the equipment to check it for frays or weak spots or any other sign that it was worn out?

There wouldn't be time to actually climb anything with everything else going on. Taryn had *promised* there'd be no human pyramid equivalent at this orientation.

"Which group are you in?" she asked.

"Red."

"Same as me." That pleased her far more than it should. But what was the harm in enjoying a little flirtation?

Beckett peered over her shoulder at her afternoon assignments. "And looks like Michael kept you with me for rock climbing, after all. I figure the plan for today will be to meet the other staff on that rotation, do an equipment inventory, and start checking out the available climbs for campers."

Michael had said something similar yesterday, but the implications hadn't sunk in. They did now.

"Are you the head rock climbing guy?" Sarah hoped her voice sounded casual.

"So they tell me. Everything around here is a cakewalk compared to Yosemite, which is where I spent the last three years in the National Park Service. If I make it through the summer without having to use my search and rescue skills, I'll be thrilled."

He was a freaking park ranger. Who'd apparently done search and rescue in California. Which meant he knew his shit. Great for the camp. Not great for her. He was liable to figure out in less than five minutes that she was green as grass when it came to rock climbing, and then where would she be?

Was it a crime to impersonate someone at a job? She had no idea. But if she was found out, no doubt it would endanger Taryn's position here. No way would the Tullys let her sister stay if they discovered the deception. And Taryn needed this job. Sarah needed Taryn to keep this job. They *both* needed out from under the cloud of Taryn's debt and irresponsibility. Failure was not an option. Which meant Sarah had to think fast or risk everything.

Beckett steered her toward the breakfast buffet. "Better eat up. It's gonna be a long day."

"Greeeeeeat."

How on Earth was she going to keep her cover?

TARYN MEADOWS KNEW her first aid. She sailed through the class, hand up, voice clear and confident as she readily answered questions. Beckett decided it was true what people said—confidence really was sexy. The legs certainly didn't hurt. And damn, he'd had dreams about those legs last night, along with those big Bambi eyes and that mouth.

As the session broke up, Michael bumped Beckett's shoulder. "Doesn't look like Heather's services as Cupid are necessary."

"Huh?"

"I see how you've been looking at her since the swim test yesterday."

Since he couldn't deny it, he only shrugged. "Just enjoying the view."

Michael smirked. "Pinecone Lodge, man. Pinecone Lodge."

Beckett gave him a friendly shove. "Shut up."

His buddy only laughed.

"Yeah yeah, whatever. I've got work to do," Beckett announced.

Over lunch, he made the switch from student to instructor, calling all of his people together at the end of the meal. "The plan for today is inventory of equipment, both ours and the gear meant for the ziplines and ropes course. And a quick tour of the most common climbing locations around camp."

Taryn's hand went up. "Might I suggest we do the tour first? It would be a nice mental break after the morning's classes and a chance to stretch our legs."

It was six of one, half dozen of the other to him. "Sure. We can do that."

Beckett took them to the trail leading to Base Camp Adventure Park, where the zip lines and ropes course were set up. They walked the length of the various activities, discussed assignments, then he led the pack back to Boulder Mountain.

"This is our primary climb site. As you can see, there are three main paths up, separated out by experience level. Nothing here is above an intermediate skillset, as the majority of campers probably will have little to no experience," he explained.

"What about experienced climbers? Don't we have a Scout Wars session later this summer?" Diego asked.

"We'll take those on a case-by-case basis. Taryn and I will be scouting prospective locations around the camp property, as well as in the adjacent state park later this week." It seemed like the ideal means of spending some one-on-one time with her to see if this attraction could potentially run both ways.

She went brows up. "We will?"

Beckett would've felt better if she'd said it with the same amused snark she'd used when she'd caught him checking out her legs, instead of that faint look of panic. Had he done something to offend her? Maybe he'd read her signals entirely wrong. Maybe she wasn't actually interested or had changed her mind. In which case, fine. He could keep this professional. "Based on everyone's applications, you've got the most climbing experience besides me." He'd verified that himself last night by reviewing the applicants assigned to him.

She just nodded, looking faintly green.

Definitely something going on there. A bad fall? Scared to get back on the mountain? *Later,* he promised himself, when they weren't surrounded by other staff.

Back at the equipment shed, he divided up the group. "I want each of you to count and check your assigned component. Make note of any prospective issues with the gear you see. Diego, you're on harnesses. Break down the count by men's and women's. Laura, helmets. Number and size." Beckett went on down the line, passing out clipboards. "Taryn, you've got the ascenders and cams, and I'll do ropes myself."

"Got it."

He pulled the first row of coiled ropes off the rack and dumped them on the table. Michael said they'd been checked at the end of last season, but Beckett wasn't letting anybody go up with equipment he hadn't inspected himself, not even for the ridiculously easy climbs around here. As he unrolled the first coil and began checking the sheath, he noticed Taryn on her phone, frowning.

"Something wrong?"

Her head shot up. "What? No." She bobbled the phone, and it bounced across the floor toward him.

He crouched to pick it up, automatically checking the screen for cracks. Not a one. "All hail the Otterbox." He handed it back to her, but not before he noted the Google search open to ascenders. He arched a brow.

Blushing, Taryn shoved the phone away. "Oh, I just remembered a particular one somebody told me about and was trying to remember what it was called."

She was lying. Right to his face, she was lying. That chapped his ass. He couldn't abide dishonesty. What he couldn't figure out was *why* she'd lie, so he let it go, keeping an eye on her through the rest of the inventory. It took a solid three hours before he was satisfied. As each of his people passed over their clipboard, he went over it, adding notations to a master list of equipment that needed to be replaced or retired. When he reached Taryn's list it confirmed his suspicions.

Disappointment flared through him, but Beckett said nothing, setting the clipboard aside. "Looks like y'all have a little extra time before dinner. Go make the most of it."

Everybody cheered. Taryn was at the head of the pack trying to get out of the shed.

"Taryn, stay back a minute? I wanted to go over some things."

Her foot hovered inches out the door before she turned back around, a too bright smile pasted in place. "Sure."

Shit. That smile was every bit as damning as the Google search had been.

He waited until everybody was considerably down the path, then shut the door. "We have a problem."

Her throat worked as she swallowed, fairly telegraphing her guilt. "We do?"

"You don't know your equipment. And if you've done more than go up the wall at the local gym, I'll go do a handstand at the top of Boulder Mountain."

Taryn just closed her eyes, resignation in every line of her body.

"How the hell did you get assigned to rock climbing?" Beckett demanded. "Did you lie on your application?"

"No. No, I—It's complicated."

He crossed his arms and waited. "Look, these may be relatively easy climbs, but I'm not having anybody out there who doesn't know what they're doing. That's dangerous to everybody involved. So you're either going to explain yourself, right now, or I'm headed to Michael and having you fired."

The blood drained from her face. "You have every right to be upset—"

"Damned right, I do."

"Look, I'll explain everything. Just not here. Will you come with me?"

Beckett frowned. "Where?"

"There's bound to be somewhere to eat in Briarsted. Let me buy you dinner and explain."

He couldn't imagine an explanation that was going to end in any other way but her being canned, but he'd liked her, so he could give her the chance to spin this away from camp. "I'll get my keys."

3

They ended up at Boone's—part tavern, part gas station, part general store, and just about the only thing on the road between Camp Firefly Falls and Briarsted, the nearest town. As it was a Sunday night and early at that, the place wasn't too busy. A handful of patrons filled booths or stood around the pool tables. Kansas played on the jukebox in the corner, and as she watched a waitress sashay by with a slice of pie a la mode, Sarah half expected to see Dean Winchester waiting in a corner. But the star from *Supernatural* wasn't hanging around with a cocky smile and a willingness to drive her away from her predicament in his '67 Impala. She'd have to find her own way out of this.

Her actual companion wasn't the friendly, easy-going guy she'd flirted with at the lake. Beckett's blue-gray eyes had chilled to flint since inventory. Sarah couldn't blame him. Nobody appreciated being lied to, and when it came down to it, he was the one responsible for the safety of both his staff and the campers those staff members would be working with. He had every right to be pissed.

Sarah didn't hesitate to order a beer. She figured she'd need it to get through this mess and explain it in such a way that Taryn still had a job to come back to. They remained silent, studying the menu, until the waitress returned. In honor of Dean, she ordered a cheeseburger. Once the waitress left, Sarah tipped her longneck back for a healthy swig, then wrapped her hands around the bottle, as if it were some kind of anchor. "I did not lie on my application."

"Really?" Beckett's sarcasm thudded on the table between them like a stone.

Sarah held in a wince. How to get through this without throwing Taryn under the bus? "The truth is, it wasn't my application." She lifted her gaze to meet his and found him staring, his own beer halfway to his mouth.

"How's that?"

Truth, she decided, *insofar as possible*. "I'm not Taryn Meadows."

"You're—" Evidently deciding he needed alcohol for the rest of this story, he drank deep. "Then who the hell are you?"

"Sarah. Her identical twin sister."

Beckett only blinked. "You're shitting me."

"Nope." To prove it, she pulled out her phone and found a recent picture of the pair of them. Taryn was a little leaner, definitely tanner, but otherwise, only someone who knew them could easily tell them apart.

He studied the picture for a long time, then turned that penetrating gaze on her. She wanted to squirm, but held still. He handed the phone back.

"Okay, so that's one part of the mystery solved. Now you want to tell me exactly *why* you're impersonating your sister?"

"Because she asked me to." Even as the words fell from her lips, she realized how lame they sounded.

His brows winged up. "This is a thing y'all do for each other on a regular basis? Having some fun, screwing with people?"

"No. Well, not since we were about twelve, anyway. And this one time in college when she forgot to renew her driver's license." *Shut up. You're not helping your case.*

"So why now?"

Why indeed?

To buy herself some time to think, Sarah took another pull on her beer. "She's caught in a difficult situation in the job she's leaving, one she's obliged to try and accommodate because of an even more difficult situation in her personal life."

"Meaning what, exactly?"

Sarah told him the story of Jax and the untenable position Taryn was stuck in. Their food came somewhere in the middle of the tale, so they ate while she talked and he listened. Other than muttering a few choice curses about Taryn's ex, Beckett stayed quiet until she'd finished.

"That sucks for her, it really does. Why didn't she just call up Heather or Michael and talk to them about it?"

Sarah opened her mouth, closed it again. *Because that would have been the responsible, adulting thing to do.* "I didn't ask. She came to me for help." Because that's what they did. Taryn fucked up, and Sarah helped her fix it.

"But you could've said 'no.'" His tone implied she should have.

"I told myself the same thing. Right up until I

said 'yes.' The thing is, I can never say 'no' to bailing Taryn out." She had a lifetime of history testifying to that fact.

"Why not?"

"I'm the oldest."

Beckett gave her a bland stare. "By how much?"

"Fifteen minutes, but sometimes it feels like fifteen years. I'm the responsible one who has her shit together. Kind of goes with the territory." Sarah realized that made her sister sound like a flake. "Not that Taryn is irresponsible. When it comes to safety for climbing or rafting or any of the other things she does, she's serious as a heart attack. It's the money management and, I guess you'd say, interpersonal stuff, where she has trouble."

He swiped his last French fry through ketchup and pointed it at her. "And yet you, with your shit together, are here doing certification training for something you're not qualified for?"

Now she did wince. "The only part I'm not qualified for is the rock climbing. And I *have* actually done some climbs that weren't in the gym. Taryn's taken me a few times, but since I started grad school, there hasn't been time. Look, she knows the handbook backward and forward. She's certified in first aid, CPR, and a whole laundry list of other things you probably saw on her application. She absolutely *is* qualified to deal with the rock climbing, and she'll be back in plenty of time to prove it. We're supposed to meet in Briarsted to swap out a couple days before the certification test at the end of orientation."

Beckett's eyes narrowed. "So you're asking what, exactly?"

"I'm asking you not to blow the whistle."

"You're asking me to lie." The hard tone told her she'd lost this battle, but she made one last effort.

"I'm asking you to wait. She needs this job. More, she desperately *wants* this job, and she'll be great at it. And if, for whatever reason, she doesn't pass the certification tests, then whatever the consequences are, they're on her. I'm just asking you to give her a chance."

Shoving the plate away, he sat back and studied her, finally shaking his head. "I won't lie to Michael. I won't pretend the person I'm working with is qualified, when she's not."

Sarah's hope withered. This was what failure felt like. Utterly wretched. It was why she didn't take risks in her own life. Why she always strove to be the best at everything she did. On top of all that, she hadn't realized exactly how much she'd wished she had a partner in crime. Or a partner at all. After being half of a duo most of her life, she and Taryn had been on opposite paths for the past several years, and she missed being half of a whole. But it really had been too much to ask for someone else to participate in their crazy. She blew out a breath. "I understand. I had no right to ask you to cover for her. For us. I'll find the Tullys when we get back to camp and explain."

"No, you won't. You're going back to camp, and we're going back to that equipment shed. And I'm not letting you leave it until you can name every-thing in there, piece-by-piece. Then tomorrow morning, you'll be up with the sun to start all over again."

She stared at him. "Excuse me?"

"I won't lie. But I'll get you certification-ready myself."

For a long moment she simply sat in stunned silence. He was offering to certify her. To go above and beyond to help her, help Taryn. "Why would you do that?"

"Much as I disagree with what you're doing, I appreciate the motivation behind it. I get what it means for somebody to give you a chance when the odds are stacked against you. Add to that, I like you." His mouth snapped shut after the admission, a little like slamming the barn door after the horses had gotten out.

He liked her. The confession caused a flutter in her chest and a bloom of heat in her cheeks. It was foolish, silly, girlish reaction. One she hadn't felt since... She couldn't remember the last time she'd been flattered and flustered at a guy's interest. Add to that, he truly was serving himself up to be her hero. It was a potent cocktail, one Sarah didn't know what to do with. As soon as her sister showed up, she was going back to New York. Nothing between them could really go anywhere. But the fact of the matter was, she liked him, too. A helluva lot.

"Thank you. Truly. My sister and I will both owe you."

Beckett waved that way. "Not worried about that. Now finish your burger. We've got a lot of work to do."

BECKETT WAS GOING to regret this. What the hell was he thinking, promising to certify an almost totally green climber so she could pass as someone more experienced? Irritation—with himself, with the situation, with her—made his movements jerky as he unlocked the equipment shed and let them inside.

You weren't thinking with your big boy brain.

Which was also ridiculous. She'd be gone in less than two weeks. Before the certification test, she'd said. Where did he think this was gonna go? Hadn't he said he was bored with casual hookups?

He blamed Michael and Heather and their absurdly infectious happiness. He blamed this place. Most of all, he blamed the fact that he couldn't bet against the underdog. He'd been one too often in his life, so he had sympathy for the real Taryn. And a helluva lot of respect for the sister who was willing to put herself out there trying to help her.

"Sit," he ordered.

She did, without complaint, waiting as he gathered up gear. That ready acceptance of whatever he was gonna dish out had his temper cooling. She was a woman who did what needed to be done. Period. And he found that way too appealing. Maybe because he understood the need to do the hard thing, regardless of personal consequences. He had a feeling Sarah knew a lot more about consequences than her sister did.

By the time he sat across from her at the work bench, he was calmer. "I'm not going to ask you what you already know. I'll teach you as I'd teach any novice."

"Okay."

He slipped into instructor mode, repeating the lecture he'd given so often to beginner classes in the past. He went over components, explained their purpose, showed how each worked together. Through it all, Sarah listened, intent. And when he asked her to repeat the details back, she did, without error.

"You're a good student."

A flash of that humor he'd caught yesterday lit her eyes. "Ought to be. I've practically made a career of it."

Oh, right. She'd mentioned she was in grad school.

Beckett picked up one of the harnesses. "Now we're going to suit you up." As he took in her expression of alarm, he added, "Not to climb tonight. Just to show you proper harness fit and begin introduction to the knots you'll be using." He held it out so she could step into it.

Hesitating only a moment, she laid her hand on his shoulder for balance and slipped one leg through, then the other. Beckett rose and worked the harness up, which pulled her nearly flush against his body. He'd been in this position countless times before, but his blood had never begun to pump like this. Her hand was still on his shoulder and her pupils dilated wide, those Bambi eyes tempting him to dive in and drown.

"Where are you in grad school?" he blurted, pulling his attention back to the harness and reaching for the waist strap, threading it through the buckle on the first side with as much business-like efficiency as possible.

Her hand fell away. "Columbia. This time."

"This time?"

A little sheepish, Sarah shrugged. "Taryn and I share an inability to settle on a career. Her response has been to move from job to job, trying out this or that. Mine has been to collect degrees."

"An expensive thing to collect." Even state colleges were hella expensive these days, and he knew well enough the cost of an Ivy League education. He was still paying his off.

"If you're a good enough student, you can get scholarships or assistantships to pay for it. I like learning things, so as long as I could stay in school without going into debt, I picked that. It seemed less scary than the real world. My sister says I'm a terrible bookworm."

She didn't fit his mental image of a bookworm.

Then again, he hadn't been the typical MBA student either.

Beckett grabbed the other side of the waist strap and threaded it through the buckle, drawing it snug. "There shouldn't be room to fit more than a couple of fingers in." He demonstrated and immediately regretted it as his fingers pressed against the flat of her belly. Just a thin layer of cotton separated him from skin. Sarah hissed a breath. He started to apologize, but instead, his eyes tracked to her mouth. Her lips were pink and glossy. He wondered if she'd taste like the pale ale she'd been drinking at dinner.

"You're supposed to...to double back the straps," she said.

For a moment, his mind blanked because his hand was still on her, and he could feel her warmth against the backs of his fingers. What were they talking about?

"And tuck them in the sleeve." Her throat worked as she swallowed.

The harness. He was fitting her for the harness.

Beckett cleared his throat. "Right. Good."

Dropping his gaze, he finished adjusting the rest of the straps, which just put him in close proximity with those excellent legs of hers. His fingers itched to touch and stroke, to find out if her skin was as soft as it looked. Jesus, if he was this rattled by being close to adjust her harness, how was he going to teach her the rest of it? Straightening, he gave her harness a few tugs, checking the fit. It would just take one pull to haul her into him...

"This is a terrible idea."

Beckett didn't realize he'd spoken aloud until she said, "Probably. But we've established I don't run from terrible ideas."

His eyes came back to hers, deep and dark and steady. Neither of them was talking about the climbing. The air between them snapped taut, shuddering like a rope under too much strain.

"Are we going to talk about this?' he rasped.

"Do you *want* to talk?" There went her eyebrow, that little sign of the sass he liked so much.

"No." If they talked about it, one or both of them would probably come to their senses, and this moment would disappear. Foolish as it was, he didn't want that.

Sarah laid a hand on his chest. "Neither do I."

To hell with it.

Beckett gave in, curling his hands around her harness and tugging her into him, until they softly collided, body-to-body. Her arms slid around his waist as she tipped her face up. Her mouth was soft, yielding beneath his on a sigh that fired his blood. Needing to touch her, he lifted a hand to cup her nape, stroking the silky skin there before angling her head so he could take the kiss a little deeper. On a sexy little moan, she rose up, opening for him. They hovered there at that delicious edge of thickening arousal, and then she dove.

She flooded his senses, the taste of her, the scent of her, wrapping around him, pulling him under, on a fast, reckless slide that burned through whatever sense remained. Blind and deaf to anything but her, Beckett shifted, backing her up until they bumped against the table. Mouth still fused with hers, he lifted her onto it. And Jesus, her legs were as smooth and toned as he imagined. She wrapped them around him, locking them at his back.

He skimmed his hands beneath her shirt, spanning the heated skin of her back. Hers followed suit, tunneling beneath his T-shirt to skate up his chest. Well, who was he to deny a lady? He yanked it off and found her lips again, glorying in the delighted purr she made as she explored his pecs and shoulders. When those fingers dug into his shoulders, he growled, and nudged up her tank top to find her pert breasts. She arched into his hands, against his hips, and he went half-mad, greedily swallowing down her whimpers of pleasure.

Before he could think—because thought had long since stopped—his hands went for the button of her shorts. And found straps instead.

Confused, Beckett hesitated, tearing his mouth away to see what the hell the impediment was. The harness. The damned climbing harness he'd *just* put on her himself.

"Call the locksmith," Sarah gasped.

Her eyes were huge, dark, and devastatingly aroused.

"Did you just quote *Men In Tights* to me?"

Breath still heaving, the corner of that kiss-swollen mouth curved. "Seems I did."

Beckett chuckled, dropping his brow to hers. The chuckle rolled into a full on whoop of laugher. "My God, you may be my perfect woman." Finding a thread of control somewhere in the humor, he tugged down her shirt and skimmed a thumb over her cheek. "But this is not the perfect setting."

Her smile was wry. "I suppose I got a little carried away."

"I'm not complaining, as I was right there with you. But your chastity belt of webbing probably saved us from crossing a line that shouldn't be crossed tonight."

Sarah sucked in a breath and let it out on a long sigh. "You're right. More's the pity."

"A pity indeed," he murmured as she slid off the table. Because he didn't care for the look of regret in her eyes, Beckett tipped her chin up and brushed a quick, soft kiss over her lips. "But hey, tomorrow's another day."

4

If Taryn's ass had not been on the line, Sarah would've packed up in the dead of night and driven back to New York out of sheer embarrassment. Without the fog of lust, she was mortified. She'd practically climbed Beckett like a tree, and if not for the harness and his own heroic restraint, she was pretty sure they'd have ended up naked on that table in the equipment shed. That was...appalling.

She didn't have issues with sex. She liked sex—or had in the dim, dark recesses of her memory when she'd last had it. But she wasn't in the habit of going to bed—or table—with men she barely knew. Okay, she'd *never* been so carried away that she'd been tempted by the nearest horizontal surface. Beckett Hayes packed quite the sexual punch. And dear God, those shoulders. Damn. Sex appeal aside, she *liked* Beckett. He was focused, dedicated, thoughtful, and he had a helluva laugh, when he cut loose. He interested her more than anyone or anything had in more years than she could count. He was temptation embodied, and for the first time in her life, her first instinct wasn't to question or wait or do anything but dive in headfirst. Like Taryn would.

And you're leaving in ten days.

That made last night a terrible idea, exactly as he'd said before they'd mauled each other. It had been unquestionably mutual. Which was the only reason she managed to make herself turn toward the equipment shed a quarter after sunrise the next morning, instead of veering toward the parking lot.

The campus was silent but for the twitter of a few birds, who didn't respect the holy rule of coffee before noise. Lake Waawaatesi was still and smooth as glass, reflecting the watercolor sky. Even in her uncaffeinated state, Sarah could appreciate that it was gorgeous. Somehow, that made the insult of being up at this hour a little bit less harsh. When was the last time she'd been somewhere this peaceful? At home, she'd be waking—unwillingly—to street construction or the honk and hum of traffic. This was better. So she paused, firing off a few shots with her camera to capture the moment for home. A snapshot of peace and tranquility.

Lights were already on inside the equipment shed. Bracing herself, Sarah pushed the door open. Beckett stood at the table, sorting through a bin of ascenders. No doubt he was rechecking her work from yesterday. A fresh wave of embarrassment hit, and with it came gratitude that he'd figured it out. If something was wrong with any of the equipment she'd been meant to inspect, she'd prefer it be discovered rather than someone getting hurt because of her incompetence.

He turned. The smile started in his eyes, more blue than gray this morning, spreading like sunrise to the lips she'd dreamed about. And that, too, was a lovely way to start the day.

"Mornin'," he said. "I brought coffee."

The sweetest three words in the English language.

Zeroing in on the to-go cups emblazoned with the camp logo, Sarah made a beeline across the room. "You might be my perfect guy."

She met his gaze as she lifted her cup, and suddenly that didn't feel like joking flirtation. It felt like unavoidable truth.

Ridiculous. It's just chemistry.

But it didn't feel like just chemistry as she leaned back against the table and remembered his lips and hands on her. Skin buzzing with want, Sarah crossed her legs at the ankles and cleared her throat. "So what's on the agenda this morning? Knots?"

"It can wait a few minutes. Drink your coffee and let your brain come online."

"Bless you." Maybe then her brain would catch up with her mouth and keep her from saying anything stupid. She sipped. "Do you regret last night?"

What? No! Coffee fail!

Beckett lifted a brow. "Do you?"

"I—" She opened her mouth. Closed it again. "Not exactly. I'm just embarrassed, I guess. I don't normally... It's been a while, and..."

He just stared at her, waiting.

Sarah's cheeks went tight and hot. "Never mind. Forget I asked. Pre-coffee brain can't be trusted."

Beckett added another ascender back to the bin. "I don't regret it, no. And I don't think we have anything to be embarrassed about."

She liked that he said "we." And yet...

Another ascender went into the bin. "You don't look like that made you feel any better."

"It did. It's just—" Sarah sighed. "We barely know each other."

Beckett nodded and stayed silent for a few moments, checking and clearing another two ascenders. "So what do you want to know? What's your minimum threshold of knowledge that will make you more comfortable with this?"

She laughed a little. "I don't know."

Abandoning the ascenders, he caged her against the table, planting his hands behind her. He didn't touch her, but Sarah was aware of every hard inch of him as he leaned in, close enough that it would barely take more than breathing to brush her mouth to his. He smelled of soap and cedar. Delicious.

"Look, I figure a spark like this doesn't come along every day. To my mind, it's worth following up to see if it fizzles or catches. So, what do you want to know?"

When you'll kiss me again. But that wasn't what he was asking. "I guess I can't say 'everything,' can I?"

Beckett's lips curved, and he stepped back, returning to his bin of equipment. "Okay. I'll start with a mini-bio. I'm originally from Myrtle Beach, South Carolina. Non-smoker. Social drinker. Coke over Pepsi. Dogs over cats. Morning person, which I hope you won't hold against me. Did my undergrad at USC, then grad school at Dartmouth, where I met Michael and Heather."

"Dartmouth?" She hoped her sincere shock didn't show in her tone. Nothing about this rugged man gave any hint of that world.

"Eh, don't be impressed. I left before I graduated."

Getting into an Ivy League graduate program was an achievement unto itself. She knew. "What were you studying?"

"I was getting my MBA."

"Really? I would've imagined—I don't know—environmental science or something."

"That would've been a better fit." He finished one bin and grabbed another. "I could have stuck it out, I guess. I was in the last year."

Sarah couldn't imagine being so close to finished and not following through. Just the idea of leaving such a thing dangling made her twitch. "Why didn't you?"

"They're big on group work in MBA programs. I found out in the middle of a presentation that my partner had plagiarized his entire half of the project."

"Oh my God. Did your professor fail you, too?"

"Nope. He just said that kind of thing happened in the real world, and I needed to get over it."

Her mouth fell open. "You're kidding!"

"Wish I was. I figured if that was what the real corporate world was like, I'd never be happy, and I wanted none of it. I walked straight out. Didn't even finish my half."

"Ballsy."

That gorgeous mouth of his twisted into a wry smile. "The word my parents used was 'stupid'. But that was later. There's a trailhead for the Appalachian Trail about a mile from campus. I packed a bag and hit the trail. By the time I made it to Virginia, I'd decided the National Park Service was my next step."

He said it casually, as if hiking what had to be around three hundred miles, give or take, was no big deal.

"You said you were at Yosemite the last three years?"

"Yeah. Stints at Conagree, Shenandoah, and Hot Springs before that."

"So what are you doing here at Camp Firefly

Falls? I'd think summer would be high season for a park ranger."

"It is. I'm not a park ranger anymore." Though his tone was easy, a muscle jumped in his jaw.

Something sensitive there. "I'm guessing that wasn't as easy a decision as leaving Dartmouth."

"Wasn't my decision. Budget cuts," Beckett grunted. "That's how I ended up here. Michael did me a favor."

That must've been the chance he'd been given. *God bless Michael Tully.*

He put the second bin of ascenders back on the shelf and grabbed two lengths of rope. "What about you? You said you collected degrees."

"Oh, well, it's possible my parents—proud though they were of the first three—might also be veering toward a different descriptor of my pursuits at this point."

"Three?"

"Working on my fourth." When he went brows up in expectation she sighed. "I've got bachelor's degrees in psychology, art, and nutrition. Right now I'm finishing up my master's degree in neurobiology and behavior."

"One of these things is not like the other."

Sarah laughed. "I love photography. I really wanted to be a photographer when I was younger, but, sadly, I have zero desire to shoot weddings or be a photojournalist, and as my parents are fond of reminding me, there's not really any other great way to make a living as a photographer. But I threw in as many photography classes as I could for fun all through undergrad. Enough that it gave me another degree."

"So the passion is neurobiology?"

Sarah thought of the thesis she was ready to set on fire. "'Passion' is, perhaps, not the right word."

"You don't like it?"

"I'm not sure you like anything by the time you get halfway through your thesis. I think despising your topic is part of the graduate school process." At least, that was what she was telling herself to get to the end.

Beckett hummed a noncommittal noise. "So you finish your master's degree. Then what?"

She thought longingly of the cabin she was sharing with Anna Garcia, a lovely girl from Arizona who was using Camp Firefly Falls as a stopover before joining the Peace Corps in the fall, and wished she were going to be here longer than two weeks. "A vacation would be nice, but a Ph.D. is the plan."

"More graduate school in a subject you just admitted you despise?"

"A career in research seems to demand it."

"Is a career in research what you want?"

The practiced answer she'd been giving her parents for years hovered on the tip of her tongue. But this was a man who'd walked away from *Dartmouth*. "I don't know what I want. Not business. I don't like that any more than you do. But I'm kinda too far down this path to jump off." Lord knew, if she changed fields again, her parents might kill her, even if they'd long since stopped paying her way.

"It's never too late to jump off."

The idea of it was simply mind-boggling. "I'm not as brave as you."

"I think you're plenty brave. Look at what you're doing here for your sister."

Sarah grimaced. "That's not brave. It's foolhardy, as we established yesterday."

"Still. Deciding to admit you're on the wrong path—if you are—" he qualified, "takes guts. It's not for me to say one way or the other. But seems to me if you're not happy doing it, if you don't get excited about going in to do the job or the class or whatever, you're probably not in the best field for you."

When was the last time she'd been *excited* about her studies? Her first semester of grad school probably. Before they'd put her through the hell classes meant to weed out those who couldn't hack it. She'd proved she could more than hack it, staying at the top of her graduate school class, but everything since then had been a grind. Especially this last semester. But if she didn't stick with neurobiology, if she didn't go on for her PhD, then what the hell would she do with her life?

Not comfortable with the direction of her thoughts, she declared, "This is way too heavy a conversation for this hour of the morning."

"Fair enough. It's time we got started anyway."

Sarah set her empty cup down. "Teach me, oh wise one. What are we doing today?"

"You're going to practice your knots, and then you're suiting up and we're going to practice falling."

As she watched him grab the equipment, she didn't think she needed any more practice doing that.

"—AND ascenders are mechanical devices used for directly ascending a rope or as a braking component within a rope hauling system, often used in rescue situations. How'd I do?"

Beckett smiled. "Perfect score."

Sarah pumped her fist, her big doe eyes lit with triumph and something else. "What do I get for my reward?"

"A reward, huh?"

Her mouth quirked into a grin. "You know I appreciate positive reinforcement."

He set his clipboard aside and moved to cage her against the equipment shed table, dropping his voice low. "I think we can come up with something."

Her hands came to his shoulders as he slid his over her backside, behind her thighs to lift her onto the table.

"I'm amenable to this kind of something."

"For every right answer, you should get a kiss somewhere new." Beckett skimmed his lips across her jaw, down the length of that lovely neck, lingering when she dropped her head back on a sigh.

"Mmm, I had a *lot* of right answers."

"So you did. It happens I have quite a few spots I'm dying to taste." He brought his hands to her breasts, brushing his thumbs over her taut nipples until her eyes went dark and molten.

"Beckett." His name on her lips was something

between a prayer and a plea as she wrapped her legs around his waist, pulling him tight against her center.

They both moaned as she rocked her hips against his erection.

"I want to finish this," he gasped. "I want you naked and under me, over me. Properly. In a bed."

"We both have very inconvenient roommates. And technically we still have all the hands-on work to do." She rolled against him, and he almost swallowed his tongue.

"I'm prepared to do all the hands on work you'll let me."

Sarah huffed a laugh that turned into a groan. "God, you have no idea how much I want that, but I meant the actual climbing. We don't have that much time."

"You can think about climbing right now?"

"I mean, mostly I'm thinking about climbing you, but I still have one or two brain cells left for the practical."

"I must not be doing this right."

A bell began to clang in the distance, signaling an end to their study session rendezvous. Beckett dropped his brow to hers. "Breakfast. How terribly inconvenient."

"Better than being caught at something *in fla-*

grante." She dropped her legs and slid off the table, brushing a kiss to his lips as she began to rearrange her clothes.

Beckett hung his head for a moment, wondering if they were doomed to bad timing the entire time she'd be here.

"How do I look?"

He glanced up to see she'd refastened her ponytail and pulled on a baseball cap. Her lips and cheeks were still flushed, her eyes bright.

"Unsatisfied."

The color in her cheeks deepened. "Well, there's time for that yet at some point."

I sure as hell hope so.

Shifting on her feet, she turned toward the door, suddenly avoiding his eyes. "I'm gonna head on so there's a gap between when we show up and so you have time to deal with... well, that." She nodded at the bulge in his shorts. "Sorry about that. I didn't mean to—"

"Sarah."

"What?"

Beckett reached out to snag her hand, gently tugging her back to him until he could tip her face up to his. "I really hope you don't think the only reason I'm helping you is because I want to get you naked. Or that that's a requirement. If that's not something you want—"

"I don't think either of us is under the delusion that I don't want you. It's just..."

"Complicated?"

"Yeah."

He got it. He really did. They had a built-in expiration date, and he couldn't blame her if she didn't want to cross that line because of it. So they'd see what happened.

Pressing a chaste kiss to her brow, he nudged her toward the door herself. "Go ahead. I'll join you in the dining hall. Save me a cup of coffee."

It took him longer than he wanted to get himself under control. Didn't help that one look at that equipment table had him imagining Sarah spread out on it naked and writhing from his tongue. But eventually, he made his way toward breakfast.

Michael was on the stage talking as he slipped in the back of the room. "One thing you'll find out fast once sessions actually start is that campers will inevitably do something stupid and get hurt. We need to be prepared to deal with as many varieties of injuries as we're able. Originally these emergency drills were scheduled for the end of the week, but there's rain in the forecast, so we're bumping them to today."

Oh shit.

"As you can see on your schedules, we're starting with a climbing accident scenario at Boulder Mountain, being run by Taryn Meadows. There will be other simulated injuries at various other points, all outlined in your packets. So finish up your breakfasts and meet out there at eight fifteen."

Sarah appeared at his side, a cup of coffee white knuckled in one hand, a sheaf of papers in the other. She handed the latter over without a word.

Michael had assigned Beckett as victim in the fall scenario. And it made sense. He had the most experience and could fake everything safely. But that left Sarah wide open in front of the entire staff. She hadn't been trained on how to stop falls yet.

Because you've been thinking more about getting into her pants than truly preparing her for the job. Good job, Hayes.

Jerking his head toward the door, they stepped out, moving around the corner and hopefully out of earshot of anybody who happened to be going in or out of the building.

"What are we going to do?" Sarah hissed. "I

can't do that. I don't want you getting hurt or into trouble on my behalf."

Neither did he. He'd agreed to put his ass on the line, so he was going to get them both through this. "Do you trust me?"

"Of course, but—"

"Okay. Then you be the victim. When you fall, I'll catch you. I'll run everything."

"But Michael…"

"I'll handle Michael. Can you do this? Are you okay doing this climb as a relative novice and falling on purpose?"

She swallowed, then nodded.

They made it through breakfast and back to the equipment shed to grab all their gear. Despite her nerves, she suited herself up for the climb, and he was satisfied to see she did it properly, with no encouragement from him. Before they walked out, he squeezed her shoulders. "I've got you."

"I know." She flashed a wan smile.

At Boulder Mountain, the staff was gathered. Beckett didn't see Michael, but he wasn't waiting around on him to start things. His friend wouldn't stop a training exercise in progress. After a few words with his climbing staff, he and Sarah got into position.

"Okay, so Taryn is going to simulate a newbie

climber who has overestimated her capabilities. Chances are, we'll see a fair bit of this over the summer. Now the rock climbing staff is trained to stop a fall before it becomes something to really worry about, but today, we're going to run a scenario where that doesn't happen and staff needs to stabilize her for transport to the parking lot, where medical personnel would be waiting."

He turned toward the rock wall. "Taryn, you ready?"

"Belay on?"

Beckett locked her into the ropes. "On belay."

She began to climb the intermediate path, and he began to pray. *Don't let her get hurt. Don't let her get hurt.*

Ten feet. Fifteen. Twenty.

"Looking good. Check out the view," he called.

"What?" She twisted her head and looked down. "Oh God."

Then came the scramble they'd discussed. But it didn't seem like she was faking it at all as she attempted to flatten herself against the rock face. Her foot slipped and suddenly she was falling.

For one instant, Beckett's heart leapt into his throat. In the next, he'd braked her fall. She bounced against the rock face. "Ow."

"You okay?"

"Fine."

Beckett hoped that was true. He addressed the staff. "Now, in this case, and hopefully in all others, rock climbing staff stopped this from becoming a problem. I'm going to lower her on to the ground, and we're going to practice stabilization."

He took the steps, explaining what was happening as he went and walking everyone through applying the neck collar and immobilizing her on a backboard. As members of his team were strapping her in, Michael tugged Beckett aside. "What are you doing?"

Here it came. He figured Michael would show up eventually.

"Running the rescue."

He kept his voice quiet. "Taryn was supposed to run it. It was supposed to be you strapped to that backboard."

Beckett jerked a shoulder. "I've got more SAR experience, and last time I checked, you made me senior staff in this department."

Michael frowned, looking more concerned than annoyed. "This wasn't about search and rescue. It was a drill. What's the deal, Beckett? Is there something I need to know? Is she not competent?"

Beckett began to sweat. This was exactly the

problem, the thing he was trying to cover up. But he didn't want to make the real Taryn look unqualified. How the hell was he supposed to explain this? He glanced back at Sarah, as if somehow she'd be able to telepathically give him the answer.

Realization dawned on Michael's face. "I get it."

Beckett's gut twisted. "You do?"

"I mean, I kinda thought you'd moved past this."

"Huh? Past what?"

"You're really into Taryn, and you're just awkward about it."

The hell? "I—"

Michael clapped him on the back. "Let me give you some advice, man. Jumping in and taking over is *not* the way to woo a competent woman. I've seen Taryn's profile. She is definitely *not* the damsel in distress type."

Beckett didn't even know where to begin processing the insult of all this. His buddy thought he was bad with women? Had apparently always been bad with women? What the actual hell was up with that? But Michael *had* inadvertently given him an answer. All Beckett had to do was throw himself under this bus to get out of it.

Fixing a perplexed expression on his face, he

glanced back toward where a team of people carefully lifted Sarah and began to carry her toward the main lodge. "I guess that explains the cold shoulder the other day."

Michael had no idea about all the extra up-close-and-personal time they'd been spending together.

"Don't worry. You've got all summer to get your game back. She'll come around."

Except Beckett didn't have all summer. Game wasn't his problem, but he had mere days left, and he didn't know if he'd be able to convince Sarah to pursue what was between them past next week.

5

As a rule, Sarah was not much of a drinker. But at the Camp Firefly Falls staff party that night, she desperately wished she could lose herself in a vat of margaritas. She didn't dare indulge. It was far too important that she maintain her cover as Taryn. That meant her wits needed to stay sharp while looking like she was imbibing. She had plenty of experience from college with covering up the fact that she wasn't drinking as much as everyone else. Someone had to be the responsible one, sober enough to take care of business should anything go awry. She'd done that for her sister and others. But never had she wished more for the dulling edge of alcohol.

After the near miss with Michael this morning,

she and Beckett had decided it would be best if they weren't jointed at the hip in front of everyone for the duration of the drills. It was ridiculous to miss him after only a matter of hours. But he was the only one here who knew who she really was. The only one she didn't have to fool. When she'd agreed to this insanity, she hadn't realized how much of a strain it would be. Pretending to be Taryn for an hour or two, or even a day, was one thing. Being her for nearly two weeks? They weren't *so* different that fooling strangers was a problem. Both competitive. Both athletic. Both with similar interests. Taryn was simply bolder. Less inhibited. And, at times, more reckless. The latter was hardly something Sarah intended to put on display here, but she was so anxious about the whole thing, every single remark from people felt like the potential for discovery.

"—think we ought to have some kind of *Love Boat* themed activity for Singles Week. What do you think, Taryn?"

Sarah fought not to jerk with guilt. Spy craft definitely was not her calling.

She shifted her attention to Charlie Thayer, a former romance editor who was taking the summer here to find himself.

"If what people are saying about Singles Week

is true, I don't know that it matters what sort of matchmaking activities you set up. Horny people will find other horny people and presumably engage in activities to their mutual satisfaction."

"I mean, yeah. But that's just sex. I'm talking about creating opportunities to make people really *connect* so that they have a real shot at meeting someone special."

Do not look at Beckett. Do not look at Beckett. But she was aware of him across the room. Knew that if she turned her head only a fraction to the right, she'd catch sight of those familiar broad shoulders in a black and white plaid shirt.

She sipped at the drink that was mostly water. "I don't know if you can orchestrate that or not. Seems like those meaningful connections either happen on their own or they don't. Trying to manipulate them would be like—I don't know— trying to make lightning strike."

"Oh, ye of little faith! I've seen it happen. Last summer, my cabinmate totally met the love of his life. Well, it turned out they'd met before, but camp brought them back together."

As Charlie proceeded to regale the group that had sprawled on the comfortable sofa and chairs in this corner of the main lodge with a recitation of how his cabinmate had turned out to be the firefighter who saved a woman's life, and how she'd come to camp after learning how to walk again, determined to embrace the life she hadn't been really living before, Sarah wasn't entirely convinced this wasn't the plot of one of the books he'd edited. Because how did two people from such very different worlds make it work? With a lot of effort and a hefty dose of apparently legitimate genius, it turned out.

Good for Hudson and Audrey.

But that wasn't normal.

And yet, as Sarah's gaze inevitably slid to Beckett, she understood that degree of wanting to do anything to make it work. No matter how things turned out for Taryn, she'd be sent away from here. From him. The idea of it made her ache.

They barely knew each other, so how was it that he'd become so important to her so fast? They had a connection. Chemistry, certainly. But there was something deeper here, and it scared the shit out of her, even as she wanted to latch on with both hands.

The very idea of it was reckless, and she was never reckless. Recklessness, thoughtlessness, that thirst for adventure and an adrenaline rush—those were all the purview of her twin. All things Sarah had never allowed herself.

But oh, she wanted to allow herself with him.

What would it harm to follow through? She wanted him. No, she wouldn't get to keep him. That would hurt. But wouldn't she regret not taking the risk even more? Maybe, for once in her life, she should take a page out of Taryn's book and reach for what she wanted. No net. No reservations. Just... want.

The idea of it terrified her. But along with that terror came a visceral excitement. What would it be like to be with someone she wanted this much? A part of her was tired of always being the cautious one, the responsible one, the safe one. Deep down, a tiny part of her resented her sister for always getting to be the reckless one. For always being the one to take the risks. Taryn could take those risks because Sarah was always there to bail her out. Who was going to bail Sarah out if she took this leap? Who was going to nurse the broken heart she'd inevitably have when this was over?

Maybe it didn't matter. Walking away from Beckett, going back to New York, was going to hurt no matter what. And if she was going to hurt anyway, then she wanted the pleasure before.

But there was the question of where. Both of them had roommates in their respective cabins. They couldn't be assured of privacy in either place.

But she'd been thinking about this off and on all day, in between various training exercises. Part of the duties for all the staff was preparing the guest cabins, giving them a clean from top to bottom, prepping new linens, and generally making sure everything was in tip-top shape before the first session began. Each staff member was responsible for a half-dozen cabins. The Tullys didn't care what schedule things were completed on, so long as they were finished by the deadline. Sarah hadn't completed hers yet, but she'd taken a look at them today during a lull. Her assigned cabins were on the row farthest away from the main lodge. They could go there.

Given some of the heated looks being passed between various other staff members, they likely wouldn't be the only ones with that idea at some point during orientation. Staff had access to do their own laundry. She could see that the sheets were fresh and washed, replaced before anyone was the wiser. The longer she thought about it, the more she liked the idea. This ruse could come crashing down at any moment. She didn't want to pass up the opportunity to be with Beckett while she could.

Finishing off her drink, she rose and wandered

over to the buffet of snacks. She felt Beckett before she saw him, though he didn't touch her.

"You okay?"

"I'm ready to get out of here." She lifted her gaze to his, letting the heat show through. "Are you?"

His pupils blew wide, and his gaze immediately dropped to her mouth. "Always. What did you have in mind?"

"We slip out separately. I'm going to complain of a headache and say I am headed back to my cabin. Give me about twenty minutes."

"Your cabin?"

Sarah shook her head, careful not to look at him. There were too many eyes, too many people who could be watching them. Under other circumstances, it wouldn't matter. But everyone here believed her to be her sister. Beckett wouldn't be involved with Taryn once the swap was made, so they had to be discrete.

"My cabin cleaning assignments are on the outer rim. Come find me there."

Heart pounding, she didn't even spare him a glance before walking back over to the coworkers she'd been sitting with. She rubbed her temples. "I've got a bit of a headache. Whiskey always does that to me. I should've known better. I'm gonna head on to bed. See you in the morning."

A flurry of concern and good nights followed this announcement. Sarah waved away any offers to walk her back, and slipped out the side door of the Lodge.

The cool of the night was welcome. Her skin felt taut and feverish. Was she really going to do this? Was she really going to seduce a man she'd known for less than a week? The deep pull of anticipation low in her belly said absolutely yes.

She stopped by her cabin to pick up a few supplies, then slipped back out again sans flashlight to make her way to the outer ring of guest cabins. The quarter moon gave just enough light that she could see. It reflected off the surface of Lake Waawaatesi and made her itch for her camera. She'd try for another shot later. Hopefully there would be time.

The cabin she chose was nestled back among the trees, the third in a row of six she'd be responsible for cleaning, and the farthest from any of the currently inhabited buildings. By her estimation, she had maybe fifteen minutes before Beckett came after her, so she'd use the time to set the stage.

The windows were closed. Each one was

screened, so they could open to the fresh air. Under other circumstances, if they had true privacy, she'd appreciate being able to hear the lap of the water on the distant shore and the call of the night birds. But they didn't have that privacy. Not now. This was borrowed time, so the windows would stay shut. Carefully, she lowered the roller shades before setting the tiny, battery-powered lantern on a side table and dialing it to the lowest setting. No reason to give anyone something to investigate.

Moving quickly, she nudged the two beds together. Might as well give them some space. The two twins together would make a king. She added fresh sheets and pillows, topping the whole thing with one of the soft, fluffy duvets. It didn't stretch to cover the sides of the shoved together beds, but they wouldn't be staying the night, and cold was hardly going to be an issue.

Her heart fluttered with every minute that passed. She didn't wonder if Beckett was coming. She knew he was. He could no more resist the pull between them than she could. She so wanted to satisfy this curiosity. Wanted to let go and enjoy as much as she could, no matter how brief a time they might have.

It was entirely unlike her, but she wasn't afraid.

Not with Beckett. He was a man who made her feel safe, no matter what. It was an appealing and attractive thing to have someone else looking out for her. For once. Hell, maybe that was part of the appeal. She'd never had that before. The sensation of safety and the inherent freedom that came with it was like a drug, and she wanted another hit. With him, she felt as if she could actually take a risk, because so long as he was there, it wasn't a risk at all.

She considered undressing, waiting for him naked between the sheets. But then they'd lose the fun of getting to strip each other. She wanted his hands on her. Wanted the thrill of feeling each layer disappear, anticipating what came after the unwrapping. So, still dressed, she sat on the edge of the bed to wait.

"DIDN'T MANAGE to dig yourself out of the doghouse, huh?"

Beckett dragged his gaze away from the door Sarah had just disappeared through to find Michael studying him over a long-necked beer in a Camp Firefly Falls koozie. "What?"

"I mean, you didn't even manage to talk to her for more than three minutes before she left. She must really be pissed about today. I'm sorry, man. I know you like her."

Was it possible for Michael to be any more wrong? Because, unless Beckett was highly mistaken, he'd just been invited to sneak away for some alone time. Prospectively naked alone time. By the very woman his friend thought he'd blown it with.

"Here. Have another beer, and we'll strategize how to fix this."

Beckett didn't want another beer, and he definitely didn't want advice on his love life from Michael, but Sarah had said give her twenty minutes. He could endure his buddy's well-meaning suggestions for that long, right?

The beer turned out to be a good idea as Michael continued to elaborate—in great detail—what had gone wrong in every relationship Beckett had attempted in grad school. Because, evidently, "We just weren't a good fit," wasn't actually a valid reason in Michael Tully's world. The recitation of his relationship faults went on so long, it was more like half an hour before he finally managed to get free and slip out of the lodge.

God, he hoped Sarah was still waiting and hadn't given up on him. Worse, he hoped she didn't think he wasn't coming.

With an eye out for other staff, he took the straightest route he could manage to the specified row of cabins. He had no idea which one she meant, but he trusted in the notion that it would be obvious when he got there.

The faint glow of light from a cabin that was the most off the beaten path was the only clue he had. Beckett made his way up the steps and hesitated at the door, wondering if he should knock. But it wasn't like Sarah would be expecting anyone else. Nobody had reason to be out here. That was probably why she'd picked it. So, he tried the door. Finding it unlocked, he let himself inside.

Bathed in the dim glow of a small, battery-powered lantern, Sarah sat at the edge of what he could only assume was a freshly made bed. A big bed that he realized was two twins shoved together. That seemed like a pretty clear sign to him.

His heart began to pound with anticipation, but he didn't rush. Instead, he quietly shut the door behind him. "Hey."

"Hey, back."

"Sorry I was late. I got dragged into conversation with Michael."

He saw the tension snap into her body. "Is there a problem?"

"No. At least not about the swap. He thinks I need help with my love life."

After a beat of stunned silence, she began to laugh, attempting to muffle the sound with her hand. "Why?"

"Well, that's partly how I covered for us this morning. He thought I took over out of some misguided attempt to impress you. Letting him keep thinking it seemed the safest way to avoid any more questions. He informed me very seriously that Taryn is not a damsel in distress sort of woman and that that was not the way to impress her."

She pressed her lips together, clearly trying to suppress a smile. "Well, he's not wrong. Thank you for throwing yourself on your sword to protect me."

Though every cell in his body wanted to touch her, he stayed where he was. "Is that why we're here?"

Her slow breath was loud in the dimness. "We're here because I want you, and this insanity could be over any day. If today taught me nothing else, it brought that point home." She lifted her gaze to his. "I don't want to leave here without being with you."

By now, Beckett knew her well enough to understand that this was a big deal for her. Because she wasn't the reckless twin. She was always the one with a plan. Always the one looking out for everyone else. And it was both exciting and humbling that she was willing to take a risk on him. On them.

So he closed the distance between them and tugged Sarah to her feet, pulling her flush with his body, where it was already wildly evident that he was on board with this plan. And yet still he felt the need to be sure, because he didn't want her to have regrets.

"Is that what we're doing? Carpe diem and all that?"

She looped her arms around his neck. "Yeah. It's outside my comfort zone, but I find that, with you, that's not so scary."

It wasn't a promise. Beckett knew it was too early to ask for any. But it was a hell of a lot more than he'd thought he'd get from her.

Her cheek was velvet beneath the stroke of his thumb. "I've got you, Sarah."

She closed her eyes at that. Not as if trying to block the words out, but as if to hold them in. To hold them close. As she relaxed against him, he wondered when the last time was that someone did have her back. Had they ever? Or had she always been the one to take care of everyone else?

Her eyes opened again. "We should probably turn out the light, in case someone sees."

"Okay." He reached over to do just that and spotted the string of condoms waiting. "You're certainly prepared."

"Pays to be. But they're part of the cabin supplies. The first session is Singles Week, remember?"

In all the certification prep, he'd forgotten. "Lucky us."

"Lucky, indeed."

He switched off the light, and they were plunged into darkness. With the shades drawn, only the faintest glint of moonlight seeped in around the edges. They'd have to explore each other by feel. Beckett couldn't find a damned thing wrong with that as he found Sarah's mouth with his. She opened for him, the taste of her flooded his brain, sparking an urgent beat in his blood. Not so much from the threat of being caught—though that was always a possibility—but more a desire to grab hold of every moment they could have together. Because they had a built-in expiration date for this thing between them, unless he could convince her otherwise. This seemed like an excellent way to show her why they shouldn't let that clock run out.

Frantic hands stripped off shirts, streaking over newly exposed flesh to explore and exploit. He fumbled off her bra and filled his hands with breasts, drinking in her moan as he thumbed her nipples. Needing to taste more, he tore his mouth from hers and bent to suck one of those delicious tight buds into his mouth as he went to work on her shorts. One of her hands dove into his hair, holding him to her as the other worked their way between them and into his jeans and boxers to close around the length of him. They both swore, bucking against each other in a desperate rush to remove the last of their clothes.

Then at last—at last—they tumbled onto the bed in a tangle of naked limbs. Gasping, their mouths fused again as they touched and took. His hand slid down the smooth plane of her belly to dip between her legs. She was hot and so very wet. Her head arched back on a moan as he drew a finger through all that heat. Aware that noise could also bring attention, he took her lips again, swallowing her cries as he slid one finger inside her and began to drive her up. He drove himself out of his mind as he felt her hips riding his hand and added a second finger to her slick, hot channel. Her muffled whimpers grew higher, her pace more fevered, until he shifted his hand again to press his thumb firmly against her clit and felt her detonate.

Glorious. She was glorious in her abandon, and he wanted more.

Even as her body continued to ripple around his fingers, she was reaching for him, curling her own hand around his cock and making him swear.

"Need you," she gasped.

She was the one who found the condom in the dark and rolled in on. As competitive as she was, he expected her to take control, to push him to his back and straddle him. He didn't give a damn how she wanted it, so long as he ended up inside her. But instead of taking the lead, she rolled, pulling him over the top of her. As he settled between her thighs, the tip of his erection nudging her entrance, she sighed with pleasure. "God, I love the weight of you."

Beckett slid the first bare inch inside her and groaned. "You feel incredible."

"So do you. Keep coming."

"That's for you to do."

On a laugh, she drew him down for another kiss, and he began to sink into her in short, shallow thrusts. Her body was so tight, but it seemed to pull him in with every rock of her hips, until her lovely, long legs were wrapped around his, holding him deep. They both moaned in pure ecstasy.

This was perfection. This was coming home. This was the thing he didn't know he was missing until this moment, when they were fully joined.

Oh damn, but he was in trouble.

Beneath him, Sarah bucked her hips, urging him to move. He slowly withdrew, only to sink in again with exquisite slowness. He wanted to draw it out. Wanted to maximize the pleasure for them both.

"Beckett, please."

"Taking my time here," he gritted out, though he could already feel her beginning to tighten around him.

She was close. But he wanted to push her higher. To brand himself on her. To make her re-member this moment. So he shifted the angle, dri-ving deeper, swallowing her gasps of pleasure as he ruthlessly kept her right at the edge of mad-ness, until his arms began to tremble from the strain and he felt the lightning gathering in his spine. Only then did he pick up the pace, stroking fast and deep.

Her orgasm struck like a storm, swamping them both. He managed to hang on through the strangled grip of her body, riding out her release before letting go and finding his own.

6

"I am so unbelievably glad you managed to coordinate this scouting trip to be overnight." Even if it did mean every step along the trail reminded Sarah of last night. Her body felt thoroughly used in the most delicious way, which made operating on single digit hours of sleep well worth it, in her opinion. "I don't know how to be around you and *not* look like I know what you feel like naked and I'm wondering how soon I can get you that way again."

Ahead of her, Beckett snorted. "Well, that wasn't precisely the motivation behind my original plan for searching out locations for the Scout Wars session, but it definitely contributed to the packing of the two-person tent instead of one.

We'll be out here all alone. No reason to be quiet."

Heat bloomed in Sarah's cheeks. "Hey, it was entirely your fault that we nearly got caught. You were the one who did that thing with your mouth that made me lose my mind." Her body clenched and shuddered at the memory, and she fervently hoped he'd offer up a repeat performance tonight.

"I'm just glad I thought to lock the cabin door and that we were able to duck into the bathroom and hide before security caught us."

"Small mercies. Though, given the stories I've heard since I got here, people being caught in compromising positions is pretty common, both among the staff and the guests."

"Totally. Charlie mentioned how there's actually a Banging Bingo game played over the course of the summer. Each square is a location and sexy situation. Everybody on staff can play, and the first person to get a BINGO gets their choice of dinner in the 5-star restaurant or a day at the spa."

Sarah laughed. "Oh, Taryn is going to love that. Hell, give her long enough, and she might co-opt a square if she finds someone she thinks is worth her time."

"She wouldn't be embarrassed by that?"

"She'd wear it as a badge of pride. I'm not sure

my sister is capable of embarrassment. None of her missteps and stumbles and failures have ever seemed to bother her. This whole mess with her ex is the first time she's ever seemed to register that there are consequences for her actions."

He stopped at an overlook, and Sarah stepped up beside him, gasping at the gorgeous view. Rolling green hills stretched out to touch the mountains that rose and fell in waves, their rocky peaks touching distant clouds. In the valley below, a glassy blue lake reflected towering pines that lined its edges. There was a sense of timelessness here. No man-made structures were visible, and it was easy to imagine this was how the place had looked centuries ago.

Automatically, she lifted her camera to capture the shot for posterity. She'd been doing a lot of that today.

"She's failed a lot?"

Dragging her brain back to the conversation, Sarah couldn't quite hide the bitter edge to her laugh. "Sometimes it's felt like that's all she's done. She skated through school, more interested in social stuff and sports than performing in her classes."

Beckett kicked back against a rock outcropping and thumbed an electrolyte chew off a roll from his pack. "Let me guess—you were top of your class."

Was she so predictable?

"Guilty. Valedictorian."

"High school is rough for a lot of folks."

"True. But college wasn't any better for Taryn. She did graduate, eventually, with a degree in multi-disciplinary studies. Which is basically the the official degree of *I don't know what I want to be when I grow up.* And even that was only after taking a couple of gap years. Since then, she's bounced around from job to job. Lots of seasonal work. A little of this. Little of that. No consistency. She hasn't stuck with anything long enough to even start something like a career."

"A career's important in your family?" There didn't seem to be judgment in his tone. Only curiosity.

"Being able to support yourself. Save for retirement. All that. Yeah. My parents are high-achieving people, and they've always worried about Taryn and her inability to stick to anything. She'll walk away from something she doesn't like at the least provocation."

"So you consider quitting failure?"

"In a sense. Failure to finish. Failure to launch. You have to finish things to be successful."

"Do you see me as a failure? I mean, I quit Dartmouth in my last year of grad school."

Horrified, she laid a hand on Beckett's arm. "Of course, not. God, please don't think I'm being critical of you."

"I don't. I'm just playing devil's advocate to figure out how you think. You say I'm not a failure for quitting. How do you square that with everything you've just said?"

"Because you didn't just aimlessly flit from one thing to the next. You got another job that you kept for however many years. You did the work. Did additional training and stuck with something until you got laid off. There's no shame in that. There was no control in it for you. No choice."

"So, the failure only comes when you make the choice?"

Sarah frowned, kicking back against a boulder and sucking on her hydration bladder as she considered. "No. That's not it either. Traditionally, failure is a matter of trying a thing and it not working."

Beckett folded his arms. "You know, I've never liked the notion of failure as a concept. That always felt wrong to me. Too much of a zero sum game. Thomas Edison technically failed in his quest to make a light bulb a thousand times before he got it right. But we don't consider him a failure. We consider him a success because he kept trying. To my mind, failure isn't a bad thing. It's just a learning opportunity. It's like... when you're learning to walk. You probably try hundreds, maybe thousands of times before you succeed. And nobody sane is criticizing babies for not becoming toddlers faster. They're just so excited the kid can walk, and then they're praising her left, right, and upside down."

"Being a grown up is not the same as learning to walk."

"Why not? It feels like a solid analogy to me. Nobody walks on the first try. They have to stumble and fall. They learn from that and adapt. Success is no different. You have to try stuff and fail to figure out what works for you and what doesn't. The whole point of life is to figure out what we want to do with it. What is our reason for being? The thing that's going to contribute to society and give us joy?"

Sarah was so taken aback, she couldn't speak for a moment. Not once had she thought about her future through that lens. Personal fulfillment wasn't exactly a catchphrase in her house growing up. "I... never considered that."

He looked down at her. "What do you think the point of life is?"

"I... don't know. My whole life, I've been driven by achievements. I've always consistently moved from one thing to the next. Always aimed for the next goalpost. I never stopped to think about what the actual *point* was. Shit, that just got deep."

Beckett chuckled. "I like deep. Here's what I see in you: You like learning. Now, if you want to continue to collect degrees, or you want to become a professor or something, because you like learning and you like the idea of teaching, that's great. That's a noble calling. But I haven't gotten the remotest impression that's what you want to do with your life. Yeah, you like to learn stuff, but I question how much of it is about learning and how much of it is about achieving? You like to win. That's been crystal clear from the moment I met you. You're smart, so staying in school, collecting those degrees was an easy way to keep winning. And I think because of that, you have a very narrow definition of failure. Because to an achieving person, not achieving is failure, not winning is failure, not finishing is failure. That's not how the rest of the world works, and I think that scares the shit out of you."

Sarah gave him the side eye as she slipped off

her pack and dug out some trail mix. "Bringing the hard truths today, huh?"

"Just calling it like I see it. I can back off."

"No. You're not wrong. Academia is comfortable to me. I understand the rules. I know the expectations. And yeah, to a point, it's easy for me, so I haven't had to confront failure as much. That familiarity is more preferable than the uncertainty of the real world. When Taryn finished school, she spent months hopping from job to job, never finding the right fit. Often going through stretches where she didn't have enough money to cover her living expenses. The idea of that instability terrified me. So I stayed in an environment where I didn't have to face that uncertainty."

"At some point, you have to leave the bubble."

"I know that. Objectively. But there's a huge difference between taking that step with a rational plan in place and just acting on impulse." She'd had a lifetime of examples of how impulsive thinking could get someone into trouble.

Beckett tugged her around until she stood between his knees. "You didn't have a plan for me."

She couldn't argue with that. "No. No I didn't."

"How's that working out for you?" There was a teasing note to his voice that made her think again about all the orgasms they'd shared last night.

She looped her arms around his shoulders. "I think you know it's working out for me very well. Even if I am walking a little funny today."

He barked a laugh. "Tell me something. Since you came up here, have you given a single solitary thought to your thesis?"

The wince was automatic. "No. But, in my defense, Taryn kind of pulled the wool over my eyes on that one. Because the idea that I'd have time to actually write and do orientation is sort of ludicrous. I didn't realize that when I agreed to this."

"Yeah, but that's two different things. Not having time to work on it is not the same as not thinking about it."

She shot him a wry smile and toyed with the hair at his nape. "I've been thinking about you."

He grinned. "For which I am eternally grateful. But seriously, if your thesis and master's degree was a thing that really, deep down, mattered to you beyond checking off a box to say 'I did that. I finished that,' wouldn't you have been thinking about it in the back of your brain, despite everything else that's going on?"

She tried to bite back the defensiveness. This wasn't a criticism. He was just making conversation. "I've been struggling with writer's block for months. The hope was that coming up here would get me unstuck."

"Well, in that light, maybe the not thinking about it will end up being productive for you. I don't know. I just don't think that you pursuing a PhD program that's going to last for years more is going to make you happy. And I freely admit that there's a selfish component in all that for me because I want you to be happy. I want to have the chance to make you happy."

His words struck her as far more serious than he probably meant them. But that didn't diminish their impact. When had anybody really concerned themselves with her happiness? The idea that this intelligent, interesting, sexy man cared enough to want to contribute to that absolutely knocked down her defenses and made her yearn.

This was all bumping up against the future and the after that they were both being very, very careful not to talk about. Because the truth was that as intimate as they'd been, and as important as they'd become to each other, they'd only known each other for a matter of days. And the idea of making a change—a significant change—in her life, for a man she knew so little, struck her as the most reckless, irresponsible thing that she could do.

And that didn't dim the wanting one bit.

Not wanting to read more into his statement than was there, she kept her tone light as she curled a lock of his hair around her finger. "Well, you're doing a pretty damned good job."

"Oh, would you look at that view." Sarah's voice was hushed and reverent, her camera already at her eye.

Watching her, Beckett smiled to himself.

Today had been amazing. Free to be themselves, without worry of being overheard or having to maintain the deception, he'd been able to get to know her on a deeper level. She fascinated him. They were very different people, and he didn't entirely understand her innate sense of competition. But she made him think. And, as always, she made him want.

He truly liked her on every possible level.

The official purpose of this overnight camping trip, at least insofar as work was concerned, was to choose appropriate locations for the Scout Wars events later in the summer. But his greater purpose had been to show Sarah all the beautiful places in the area to feed her inner photo bug.

She'd told him that she'd wanted to be a photographer in a way that said she hadn't ever *really* considered it a viable career option because of her parents. Yet she'd loved it enough to keep taking classes, keep learning about it. And certainly she'd kept shooting. He hoped that by bringing her to a lot of his favorite places out here, she'd have a chance to indulge that love. And maybe he'd find a way to help her consider it as an actual profession. Because he saw the light in her when she had a camera in her hands that he hadn't seen when she'd discussed any of the degrees she'd earned.

The quiet click of the shutter was background noise as he slid off his pack and began to make preparations for camp, digging out the tent.

When she saw what he was doing, she started to put the camera down. "What can I do?"

Beckett waved her off. "I've got this. You keep taking photos. You're having such fun with it."

Sarah flashed him a giddy sort of smile and turned back to her work. That smile was worth every mile they'd hiked today.

He unfurled the tent and stretched it out on the grass. "What is it you love about taking pictures?" He was legitimately curious. Photography was such an artistic thing, and every other degree she'd sought had been so painfully rigid and scientific. He was still trying to square the two sides of her.

She seemed to consider the question. "There are beautiful things in the world everywhere you look. I love being able to capture that. To show people there's a different way to look at things. I love the challenge of getting the shot that I envision in my brain, making people see things that I see. And I love the ability to capture a moment in time—a memory—and pull it out later to relive. There's magic in that." So saying, she lifted the camera again and aimed it toward him.

Click.

"There's an element of comfort to it, too, I guess. It's soothing. The camera is an extension of my hands. I mean, there's still thought involved in settings and angles, in the consideration of all the technical aspects, but it's not the same as being actual work."

"Do you feel like something that isn't hard somehow matters less? That because you find it easy, and you're not having to work at it, that makes it something that you don't actually want to pursue?" He legitimately wanted to know. Was her deeply ingrained sense of competition really that much of a driver for her?

She crouched to take a shot of a cluster of

purple coneflowers at the edge of the clearing. "No. It's just not a practical job."

"You talk a lot about that. About the practical. Why the obsession?"

Her brows drew together, and Beckett hoped he hadn't crossed some line. He didn't want to offend her, he just wanted to know the answer.

"One of us had to be practical growing up. By default, that ended up being me."

Beckett chose his words more carefully. "That doesn't sound like a choice."

Her shoulders twitched in a shrug. "My sister made the choice for me. Because she never stopped to think and consider before making any sort of decision. She just leaps feet first, and damn the consequences. She's always been able to do that because I was there to help manage them. And there were always consequences."

There was both love and exhaustion here, and Beckett was starting to understand how much being a twin had impacted her. He didn't think her obsession with perfection was necessarily actual temperament so much as reaction to a lifetime of being the more cautious one. As they worked together to set up camp, she told him more stories. The picture she painted was of a twin who was not at all afraid of action or of failure. Yeah, Taryn had made some bad decisions and had some crappy things happen to her as a result of that. But the end result was that Sarah had never been given the freedom to feel as if she could make a mistake because Taryn had the market cornered. It made Beckett realize that it was an even bigger deal that she had decided to take a chance on him.

He hurled the weighted end of a rope through the fork in a tree above and tugged to set up a line where they could hang their food overnight, out of reach of any bears in the area. "I'm starting to see how this thing with me, with us, is really out of character for you. And I am so incredibly grateful you were willing to take that leap with me. But I'm compelled to ask... Why did you?"

He knew he was pushing, hoping to nudge her into admitting that she also couldn't bear for this to be over after this week. That she was willing to pursue this thing between them further.

She was silent for a while as she gathered wood for a fire. When she finally spoke, her voice was low. "Because the idea of not pursuing it felt like a bigger risk than being with you. Not knowing would've haunted me a whole lot longer than whatever the fallout is after."

It was something. Maybe not as much as he wanted, but he realized that what he wanted was an awful lot in a very short span of time. Twin impersonation aside, she was a demonstrably cautious woman. So he would take what she offered and be grateful. And hopefully, somewhere in the time they had left, he'd find the key to unlocking her reluctance and grabbing onto this with both hands the way he wanted to.

He crossed over to where she knelt by the ring of stones for their fire pit and reached for her hand. When she laid it in his, warmth and electricity shot up his arm and into his chest. He drew her to her feet, pulling her flush with his body. She flowed into him without hesitation. Beckett loved that. Loved the instant surrender. The sensation of a click, as if they fit together like two puzzle pieces. Seeing the same wanting he felt reflected in her big Bambi eyes.

Linking his hands behind her back, he dropped his brow to hers. "Then let's make the most of it."

7

I'd like to schedule a meeting ASAP to get an update on your thesis. And I know you took time off, but I really need you back in the lab.

Sarah stared at the text that had come in from Dr. Osborne, her thesis advisor. It had hit her phone almost as soon as she and Beckett had returned to camp from their scouting trip. She hadn't actually responded yet because... well, she didn't know what exactly she was going to say. That left her unsettled. This entire trip was supposed to have given her clarity so she could go back and finish writing the damned thing in time to defend before fall semester. Instead, she'd met a man who had her questioning everything.

"You can see we've got some more challenging climbs here." At the front of the room, Beckett went over the sites they'd scouted with the rest of the climbing staff, marking positions on the topographical map of the area that took up one wall.

From her position in the back, Sarah pulled the memory card from her camera and popped it into her laptop. She'd taken photos of all the sites and wanted to be able to pull them up should he want them. As row after row of RAW files loaded on her screen, she winced. Finding those specific images would be a challenge. There were hundreds of shots here to comb through. Even before their trip into the state park, she'd been carrying her camera everywhere because the area was too gorgeous not to take advantage, and she'd been having so much fun getting to shoot again.

When had she stopped? Certainly, she'd done the same thing during her first few months in New York. But the stress of being in the city, studying, and all the things associated with being a success in an Ivy League master's program had forced her to set it aside. She hadn't realized how much she'd missed it. Beckett had helped remind her why she loved it so much, and in doing so, had reawakened that dream she'd dismissed so long ago, of finding a way to do this as a career.

That was a dangerous headspace to be in just now. The change of pace from coming up here was supposed to break the months-long writer's block so she could move forward. Because moving forward was simply what she did. Always.

For every random job and thing that Taryn tried and bailed on, Sarah had always felt she had to prove she could finish something. As if they were two halves of a whole in the worst possible way. As if she had to balance out her sister's poor choices and experimentation. As if she had to be perfect at everything.

Finish Master's. Get PhD. That was the plan. In the beginning, when Sarah had set out on this path, more school had been the obvious conclusion. A doctorate was the penultimate achievement. The challenge of that had excited her. But now?

While she still found the material interesting, the idea of spending the rest of her life with all the data and numbers filled her with dread instead of exhilaration. And that was terrifying. Because what if Beckett was right? What if she wasn't meant to get this PhD? If she didn't do that, then what came next?

Well, a job, obviously. But she had no idea what sort of jobs were available with just a Master's in neurobiology. Chances were they'd include all the things that were no longer exciting to her about the PhD track.

Which meant... what? That she'd wasted all her time on these degrees? That after all her big talk to her sister about the importance of finishing things, that the things she'd finished weren't actually getting her any closer to a career than the impulsive, somewhat itinerant job-hopping that Taryn had engaged in? The mere idea of it made her queasy and felt like failure in its own right.

Sarah didn't *do* failure.

"—will do a group trip for all the staff to make those climbs when we get closer to the Scout Wars session. The participants that week should have a lot more training than the average camper, but I want everybody familiar."

Plans were being made about the rest of the summer. Plans she wouldn't be around to see. The clock was ticking, and Sarah was painfully aware that her time at Camp Firefly Falls was drawing short. She was doing the job, following through on all the trainings and other work of orientation. And she had to admit that she'd enjoyed the change of pace. She'd enjoyed everything she'd done up here. It was the first time since she'd left for college that she hadn't been in active classes doing work toward an academic goal.

If she'd taken any time at all to breathe before now, would she have changed her mind about what she wanted? The notion of it left her uncomfortable. That made it seem as if her whole life was merely a product of momentum and inertia. But wasn't that how lots of people lived life? They got on a path that became a rut and often didn't pause to consider whether it was the *right* one unless something outside themselves forced the issue.

Beckett had been that for her. Because of Taryn, yes, but it was him who was making her question everything. She stopped her scroll of images on a shot of him on the trail, looking supremely at ease and in his element. An element he might not have found if he hadn't walked out of that MBA program.

You have to leave the bubble sometime.

His words played through her head again. Was it finally time to get out of school and figure her life out? Maybe. As he continued to go over details with the rest of the staff, she found herself wishing there was some way she could stay up here for the summer after Taryn finally arrived. Was there any kind of a job she could get here at this late date?

It hardly matter if there was. Letting everyone know that there were two of them would undoubtedly expose their subterfuge, and Taryn needed this job. But, God, Sarah wanted the chance. She wanted the time to spend with Beckett. She wanted more time away from her thesis. Which was reckless as hell. She was the responsible twin. The idea that she'd choose a guy over finishing her thesis, finishing her degree, was patently absurd.

What did she gain from that choice?

A lot of really great sex? Yes.

Great conversation? Absolutely.

The chance to find out if he was the one?

The question made her brain grind to a screeching halt and her heart start to pound.

They barely knew each other. And yet she felt closer to Beckett after little more than a week than she did people she'd known for years. She'd felt strongly enough that she'd leapt into bed with him, without regrets.

Was it the lust talking?

No. It was more than that. He interested her. He challenged her. And he was putting himself on the line for her.

No one had ever done that.

Then again, no one had ever needed to.

All she knew for certain was that she needed more time with him. Which was exactly why she wanted the summer. To give them time to find out if this connection between them was the kind that could last.

But she didn't see how it was possible. Because of the sister who was the whole reason Sarah had even met Beckett. So that she finally stood a chance of crawling out of the hole she'd landed in. Taryn had to come first in this. Which meant in four days she'd be going back to New York.

A band tightened around Sarah's chest at the thought. But no matter how much it was going to hurt to leave him, she wouldn't have traded this time for anything in the world. Even if he was making her panic about the plan she'd been perfectly fine with two weeks ago.

Maybe, after all this was over, it was time for her to start making decisions about her life purely for herself instead of running it all through a lens of what it would mean for her sister. In which case, she had a lot she needed to figure out.

The end of everything was coming, and that meant decisions had to be made.

Knowing she had to say *something,* she toggled over to the text thread with Dr. Osborne and tapped out a reply.

Sarah: **I'm so sorry. I'm out of town for the rest of this week. Can we meet when I get back next week?**

Before she could change her mind, she sent it.

A meeting would be good. Maybe it would give her some more clarity. Maybe she'd step back into the lab and it would feel like coming home and this whole couple of weeks would be some kind of dream. Or maybe she'd feel it in her bones that this was where she was supposed to stop. She could discuss potential job options with a terminal Master's degree with Dr. Osborne. Not that the program she was in *was* a terminal Master's. The degree was just a checkmark on the way to that PhD. Nobody just stopped there.

But she was considering it.

Already she could imagine the look of profound disappointment on her mentor's face.

Shoving the thought aside, Sarah looked up at the man she was rapidly falling for and wondered if she'd be brave enough to make a different choice than the one she'd mapped out.

Beckett loved summer storms. To his mind, nothing beat a good thunderstorm for driving people inside and encouraging naps—or other horizontal activities. Not that Sarah was cooperating on either front, just now. She stood at the doorway to his cabin, looking out at the torrential downpour that had granted them an unexpected reprieve from all the hard work of the week. The other staff had mostly holed up at the big lodge for games. Those who hadn't were ensconced in their own cabins, making the most of their leisure. He knew what he'd rather be doing with his.

"Will you come sit down?"

"Are you sure we can't head down to the equipment shed? Do some more drills or something? I hate to waste practice time."

It could never be said that Sarah didn't take her tutelage seriously. Beckett had never enjoyed teaching someone as much as he'd enjoyed teaching her. She was bright, interested, always attentive. And he sure as hell wasn't going to complain about getting to put his hands on her at every available private opportunity—many of which he'd gone out of his way to orchestrate.

"Honey, you've conquered Boulder Mountain and passed every demonstration and oral quiz I've thrown at you." She had, in fact, excelled at every single challenge he'd come up with. She was a natural. "You've earned a break. C'mere." Beckett patted the bed beside him.

With one last glance out at the rain, Sarah slipped off her sandals and flopped down on the mattress, frowning.

"That is not the expression of a woman happy to be in my bed."

Her lip quirked into a half smile as she gave him the side eye. "I'm sorry. I just can't settle. I'm worried about the certification."

Beckett stroked a hand down her arm and laced his fingers with hers. "You're not the one who has to take the test." It was as much a reminder for himself as for her.

He didn't want to think about the fact that he'd be spending the summer seeing a woman with her face who wasn't her. In between all their staff duties and training sessions, they'd talked endlessly about everything under the sun. The intensive one-on-one time had done nothing to dim his interest or diminish his certainty that there was really something here with this woman.

And in less than a week she'd be walking away.

"Yeah, but I'm in it now. I have to finish the training, have to be ready."

"Just in case?"

On a sigh, she rolled toward him, snuggling

against his chest. "Mostly just to prove that I can be."

"Because everything's a competition."

Sarah hummed in agreement and slipped a hand under the edge of his T-shirt, tracing little patterns on his side.

Beckett tightened his arms around her. He couldn't wrap his head around that worldview. "Does it come from being a twin? This competitive streak? Were you and Taryn always trying to outdo each other growing up?"

"Some. But a lot of times, the competition is with myself."

He tipped his head down to study her. "What are you trying to prove?"

She considered the question. "I don't know. When I was younger, I think some of it was to prove that I wasn't like Taryn. That I could stick things out, finish stuff. Then I guess I got addicted to winning. I like knowing I can push myself to do better, be better."

"Admirable," he conceded. "But exhausting, I'd think."

"Sometimes."

"I think there's a place for competition and sticktoitiveness. But it's not everything. Some things shouldn't be finished. Fights. Brussels sprouts. Things that don't make you happy." Beckett shifted her closer and rolled so she stretched out atop him, pleased when she dropped her knees to either side of his hips. Maybe they'd get to some of those horizontal activities after all.

Sarah folded her hands across his chest and propped her chin on them. "Didn't it bug you? Walking away from your MBA, when you were so close to done?"

He didn't even hesitate. "No."

"Really? I mean, you were that close to done. Why not finish? That was a very expensive lesson. There's not really any other point in an MBA."

He shrugged. "Yeah, but the debt was already racked up. I was never gonna go into corporate to help pay it off because it just wasn't gonna make me happy and would have done serious damage to my mental health. Having the degree wasn't going to do me any good, and I wasn't racking up additional debt by leaving."

"But if you'd stayed and finished, you would have at least had the degree in your back pocket, just in case. Because sometimes it's not about what degree you have. It's about having degrees. Proving that you can finish things."

And they were back to this again.

"Sometimes. But that's totally sunk cost fallacy.

That somehow continuing on the wrong path is justified because of the existing investment in time and money. But that doesn't make it less wrong in the end." He absently stroked the soft skin of her thighs. "In any case, I don't think I'd have realized that an MBA and that whole corporate thing wasn't for me without doing it. So in that sense, it wasn't a waste. I loved working for the National Park Service."

Sympathy shone in those big, doe eyes. "I'm sorry things turned out like they did."

It was harder to feel that way himself when he was here with her. "Eh, it's a hard job. Harder than most people realize. People think it's all hiking and climbing and doing fun outdoors stuff. It's also rescues and being law enforcement and dealing with deaths and drugs and a million other things that happen under the surface, behind the scenes. I was headed toward burning out there, too." Another three years, maybe five, he'd have been ready to move on.

"So now what?"

"I don't know. That's what I'm here to figure out this summer." But it had been her occupying his thoughts, instead.

He'd been wracking his brain for days, trying to figure out the best way to convince her that they should pursue this. Hell, he'd even gone so far as to wonder what the hell kind of a job he could get in New York after summer was over. Would being in the concrete jungle for a prolonged period kill him? Would all that be worth enduring for the chance to see where this thing between them could go?

The irony that he was considering making major changes to his life because of a woman wasn't lost on him. Sarah wasn't even his girl-friend. She'd made him no promises beyond this week. They were in a situationship, he supposed. Yet he hadn't felt this much for the woman he'd asked to move across the country with him. So how could he let her just walk away without trying for more?

Sarah sighed, her chest rising and falling against his. "I envy that. Having time to breathe, to think."

Beckett tucked a lock of her blonde hair be-hind her ear. "You could take the time." He wanted her to take it. He wanted her to take it here, enough that he was prepared to talk to Michael about hiring her on. But that was getting ahead of things.

"I have a very tight schedule to finish my thesis." She said it with the ease of a well-rehearsed excuse.

"The thesis for the degree you're not sure you like, to go on to the PhD you aren't sure you want."

Her expression turned mulish, and he knew he'd probably pushed too far. But there was so little time to convince her.

"I'm just saying—that's a lot of years to invest in something you're not passionate about." The idea of it made him shudder. Being trapped like that would kill him. Sarah wasn't him, but he could see the cost down the road of her stubborn insistence about finishing what she started. "What's the worst that could happen if you took the time to make sure it's what you really want?"

"If I don't roll on into the PhD program this fall, I might not get in. I might miss my chance."

Was it an epic case of FOMO or fear of the real world?

"Did it ever occur to you that if you took the time and didn't get in after this, that maybe you're supposed to do something else?"

"What? Like fate or God intervening?"

"I don't know. Maybe. I just think the universe tends to set us on the right path, if we're paying attention. But it's easy to get distracted by other stuff instead of listening."

"And you're here to listen this summer."

"That's the plan."

She frowned, clearly flummoxed by the idea. "How do you deal with not knowing what comes next?"

"I've learned patience." Though she was testing it. He'd been listening all week and knew what he thought was next, at least with her. But she wasn't on the same page. Not yet anyway. And he had limited time to convince her.

"Patience is not my strong suit," she admitted.

He'd pushed her far enough for one day. "Then how about distraction instead?" He stroked his hands higher up her thighs, beneath the hem of her shorts.

Sarah hummed low in her throat and wiggled in a way that had the blood draining out of his head. "I think I can get behind this kind of distraction. Except for the fact that your roommate could come back at any moment."

"There's considerable entertainment to be had without losing a stitch of clothing." He maybe hadn't engaged in any of it since college, but he'd take what he could get. Curving his hands around the firm cheeks of her perfect ass, he grinned at her. "How do you feel about baseball?"

8

"I know your secret."

At the sing-song voice, Sarah froze, her mug of coffee halfway to her lips. Panic scorched through the lingering vestiges of sleep, and she fought not to react, not to look toward Beckett for support. With herculean effort, she arched one brow in vague interest and glanced at the speaker.

Diego grinned at her from across the breakfast table, looking like the cat that ate the canary. Did he really think this was a joke? She—and Taryn— were going to get into so much trouble. Damn it. Damn it! She'd known this was a terrible idea. Known there was no way she'd really pull this off.

And how the hell did he find out? Had he overheard some conversation with Beckett? They'd been so careful.

On a yawn, as if she couldn't possibly care less, she cocked her head. "Oh yeah?"

Diego's smile spread wider. "Taryn and Beckett sitting in a tree. K-I-S-S-I-N—"

Diego's song ended in a laugh as Beckett hurled a muffin at his head. "Can it, Acosta. What are you, ten?"

"I'm just sayin', boss man, you two ain't fooling anybody, making goo-goo eyes at each other when you think nobody's looking. There's no prohibition on staff relationships, so I don't know what the point is of all the lousy attempts at discretion."

Sarah released a slow, controlled breath. He didn't know. The secret was still safe. But it brought up another question. If everybody knew she and Beckett were involved... what was he going to do when the real Taryn showed up? The idea that he'd just swap from one of them to the other had her hand clenching around the mug.

Stupid. Beckett wasn't that kind of guy, and Taryn wouldn't poach.

Not that they'd actually discussed what the hell they were doing. They'd defined nothing. This week had been all about indulging attraction and flirtation in the moment. She hadn't wanted to discuss anything else because... she hadn't come up here for this. This was a break. A moment out of normal time. A situationship. But in forty-eight hours, Taryn would arrive, they'd swap places, and Sarah would go back to real life in Brooklyn. Back to the noise, the traffic, the congestion, and the slow, suffocating horror of the city.

She'd shoved back from the table before she even knew what she was doing.

"Hey!" Diego protested. "I was just kidding around, Taryn. I didn't mean anything by it."

Holding up a hand to stop whatever else he was going to say, she just shook her head. "No. It's not... I just... I need to go." In a dozen long strides, she made it to the door, shoving through with more force than necessary to get out into the clean mountain air. It wasn't enough to alleviate the pressure in her chest. Turning toward the lake, she broke into a run, needing to put space between herself and this whole charade. To be... herself... for a little while.

Her feet thudded on the dock, echoing the thrumming of her heart as she loped down the length of it, past the boathouse, to the very end jutting far out into Lake Waawaatesi. She stood

there, breathing hard, still vibrating with a rest-
less, panicked energy, wondering if she should just
dive in and keep swimming. Like she could
somehow escape this... *dissonance.*

Everything had gotten out of hand. This hadn't
just been a job, something she could slip into and
out of with no consequences. It wasn't just a break
—it was breaking her.

"Sarah."

Beckett's quiet voice murmuring her name—
her name—had the ache and the panic coalescing
into a knot in her throat. She squeezed her eyes
shut against the burn of tears. She was fine. She
just needed to get her head on straight, so she'd
make it through the rest of this week. If she kept
repeating it, she'd start to believe it.

"Sarah, honey." At Beckett's hands on her
shoulders, she broke, turning into him and
pressing her face to his broad chest.

He pulled her close, brushing a kiss to the top
of her head. "Hey, what's all this? What's wrong?"

"Everything. I was *fine* before. I knew what I
was doing. I had a plan and a life. A good one,
damn it. This whole trip was supposed to be just
a blip. A chance to help my sister and get out of
the city to clear my head so I could get back to
work and get on with my life. Then I came here

and there was you and this place, and I can breathe for the first time in I don't know how long, and I don't know how to go back to before. I don't know how I can just up and act like this time didn't happen, and it's all your fault." She thumped his shoulder with one balled fist, but there was no real heat behind it, just a boatload of frustrated misery as she continued to let it all spill out.

"How can I go back to Brooklyn and focus on my thesis, when a big part of me is going to be here, thinking about you? How can I go back to my normal when you've planted all these questions in my head? I *doubt myself*. I never doubt myself. I always have a plan. I always know what's next because the alternative is falling into absolute, hot-mess chaos like my sister, and I will not be a hot mess, Beckett. I just won't."

She looked up at him then, shocked and not a little incensed to see one corner of his mouth twitching. "This is not funny!"

He sobered, shaking his head. "No it's not." One big hand came up to cup her cheek, a callused thumb wiping at her tears. "You don't want to walk away from us?"

Sarah stared at him. "That was your take away from all that?"

"To my mind, it's the most important part. Everything else is just details."

"Just details? How the hell do you think this is going to work? Because I've been wracking my brain for days, and I can't see a way. You're here. I'm going to be there."

"If you're determined to go back, then we do long distance for the summer. I get days off. It's not that far to New York from here. You'll want to get out of the city again. We can make it work." He stroked her cheek again. "This is worth finding a way."

She wanted to lean into the touch, into his calm assurance that things would be fine. But how did he *know*? "But what about after? You don't even know where you'll be after this summer."

"There are jobs in New York."

Equal parts moved and horrified, she shook her head. "I can't ask you to do that. You were a park ranger. You do search and rescue and rock climbing. You'd hate the city. Hell, I've been there for three years, and I hate it too. All the people and the noise—" She shuddered.

"You don't have to go back."

She dropped her gaze. "I do. I have a meeting with my thesis advisor next week."

If he felt some kind of betrayal that she hadn't

told him before, he didn't show it. But maybe he didn't realize it hadn't been set before the camp training.

"I get that you need to finish your Master's degree. At this close, I don't blame you, even though it's not the choice I made myself. But are you really willing to endure another four or more years of living with the crowds and the noise to get a PhD? Is that actually going to make you happy? Will it fulfill you?"

No. The answer trembled through her in a whisper she didn't want to hear but couldn't ignore.

"I can see the answer in your face. You don't want the PhD. You don't want the city. And that's completely fine. What will make you happy and fulfill you?"

"How can I even answer that? That makes it sound like I have everything figured out, and it turns out I've got nothing at all figured out. School, academics—that's what I know. What I'm good at."

"But it's not the only thing you're good at. I've seen your pictures. You're good."

Jerking her shoulders, she stepped away to pace. "It's not a job. It's not stability and the ability to pay my bills. I won't be burden to anyone."

"First off, I don't think you'd ever be a burden.

You've got too much work ethic for that. Second, there's a great big range between wildly successful and destitute. You are a good photographer. And there are ways to build a following, gain exposure to do things other than shoot weddings. I know a guy from my time in Yosemite who started a really nice little side hustle with stock photos. It's a passive income stream that you can continually build on."

"He had Yosemite to shoot." Probably any idiot with a camera could take good shots of that kind of glory.

"He did. But his bread and butter wasn't that. It was the small stuff. Detail shots of all kinds of things in nature and whatnot. Animals. Flowers. People. I'm sure there's some kind of logic behind what really moves in stock photos, and I don't claim to know it, but it's certainly something worth looking into." Stepping into her path, he skimmed his hands down her arms and laced his fingers with hers. "My point is, if you'll take off those blinders that have kept you focused on academia all these years, you'll find another way. A way to financially support yourself doing something that isn't going to kill your soul. Maybe it'll take a while to build and figure out, and maybe you'll have to work some imperfect jobs in the meantime, but I promise you, it's worth it."

She wanted to believe him. Wanted to believe there was a way. And yet...

"Do you have any idea how scary this is for me?"

He dropped his brow to hers. "As scary as the idea of letting you walk out of my life."

Sarah's heart squeezed hard, and there went that knot in her throat again. "Oh."

"I believe in you, and I believe in us. Maybe that's crazy after less than two weeks, but there you have it. Let's give ourselves the chance to figure the rest out."

Standing at the end of the pier, far out over the water, Sarah did the impossible. She let go of the plan that had been guiding her life for a decade and grabbed on to Beckett instead. "Okay."

"The end of orientation is coming up in a couple of days, so today the goal is to focus on team building. This year, we've elected to do that through a massive game of capture the flag." Heather's breakfast announcement was greeted with a chorus of cheers around the room.

Team exercises weren't at all what Beckett wanted to be doing on his last full day with Sarah, but he was out of viable excuses to keep them out of the mainstream activities. This was camp tradition, apparently.

"You will all stick to the teams you've been assigned from the beginning. It will be up to each team to decide who defends and who is on flag retrieval duty. Now, winners—by which I mean whichever team manages to capture and hoist the flag of any opposing team at their home base—will be first in the rotation for time off. We thought that might make for a reasonable incentive." Heather grinned, her eyes sparkling with devious energy.

"Well, that just made this a cut-throat competition," Charlie muttered.

"Teams have half an hour to convene and choose a base camp within this designated area." She gestured to the large map projected on the wall. "Team leaders can come collect your flags up here on the stage."

As designated red team leader, Beckett collected their flag before they all reconvened in the climbing hut to strategize. As it was more than merely his climbing staff, the little building was packed.

"We ought to have an advantage over everyone else," Diego insisted. "We know all the territory around the ropes course, the climbing wall, and all the hiking trails in between."

Sarah bounced on the balls of her feet, gaze tracking over a map spread out on the table. "I propose we establish base here." She tapped a finger on the map. "There's a ropes course platform right here that would give a perfect view of anyone coming. Easily defensible."

"Is that within the rules?" Laura asked. "Feels like cheating."

"They didn't expressly say we had to make it easy to get to." Sarah's eyes sparkled with the glint of competition, and Beckett had to admit to himself that seeing her this charged up was sexy as hell.

He came to Sarah's defense. "Well, considering that I'm pretty sure blue team is setting up on the swim raft out in the lake, I think we have every right to use one of the ropes course platforms as base."

They spent a few more minutes discussing duties, deciding where their "jail" would be. Then they split off into defensive and offensive forces. By the time the air horn sounded, signaling the start of the game, everyone was in position.

"So which flag are we going after?" Laura asked. "Green seems the most accessible over by the archery range. And yellow isn't too much harder, on the tennis courts."

Sarah folded her arms, her eyes narrowed as she stared out at the lake where the blue flag fluttered in the breeze at the top of the lifeguard chair on the floating island. "We're going for blue."

"Blue!" Diego stared at her. "Are you nuts? That's the hardest, by far!"

"Which is why no one else will be going for it," she reasoned. "They're cocky. See how few people they left guarding it?"

"Props for ambition, girl," Charlie put in, "but it's impossible to approach undetected. They'll tag any of us out and stick us in jail before we have time to get anywhere."

Beckett met her gaze and understood. "It's nearly impossible, but not entirely for someone who can swim like her. How long can you hold your breath?"

Her smile spread slow and wicked. "Long enough. I just need a distraction."

She approached the entire thing like a five-star general planning an offensive. Beckett had to admit, she was a good tactician. Everybody fell in line. Diego, Charlie, Laura, and the others all split up to sneak into the boathouse. They'd be attempting approaches via kayak and canoe and would hopefully serve as adequate decoys while Sarah approached from the rear.

Keeping close to buildings for cover, Beckett and Sarah made their way around to the opposite side of the lake. It was a much farther swim from this angle than it was from the dock. As she stripped down to her swimsuit, he studied the distance.

"You sure you can make this?"

"Positive. And, in the event that I get tagged and put into jail, I'm relying on you to come rescue me."

And wasn't that progress from where they'd started?

Beckett caught her in a fast kiss. "Always."

With one last grin, she slipped into the water, quickly sinking below the surface, so that only the top of her head was visible. When she started sucking in deep lungfuls of air, Beckett frowned.

"Seriously, how long can you hold your breath?"

"Three minutes, easy. Longer, if necessary."

"Can you really make it that far, that fast?"

She settled her goggles in place. "My college swim coach was a former Navy SEAL. Trust me.

I've got this." With one last, gigantic breath, she disappeared.

Beckett automatically began counting as he lifted his binoculars and watched the raft. She was right. They were cocky, and every single one of them was paying attention to the rest of the red team, who milled about in kayaks attempting to approach the raft. Some of the blue team was also in the water, serving as the police force to keep would-be thieves away from their home base. No one was paying attention to the back side.

Still counting, Beckett kept his eyes on the surface of the water for any disturbance that signified her progress or any unexpected distress. At three minutes, he hadn't seen a single sign of her. At four, he toed off his shoes, prepared to call the whole damned thing off and go in after her. Then he saw a slight disturbance of the water at the edge of the platform and a head bobbed up.

Beckett released the breath he'd been holding with a woosh.

Christ, that had been nearly four-and-a-half minutes.

Sarah stayed where she was, probably gripping the underside of the raft as she waited for the rest of the distraction to click into place.

Assured she was okay, Beckett gave the signal,

and Charlie nobly threw himself on his metaphorical sword, making a direct run at one of the blue team members and getting tagged. But he didn't go to their jail at the edge of the dock without a fight. Diego and Laura went to attempt to rescue him, and the whole thing turned into a laughing, splashing battle with the remaining blue team guards.

No one was paying any attention to the back of the raft, which was bobbing in all the chop created by the distraction. Beckett watched as Sarah smoothly hoisted herself up out of the water and onto the edge of the platform. She crouched there for a moment as the rest of their team made an even bigger brouhaha on the other side. Utilizing their distraction, she climbed the two rungs to the top of the lifeguards chair and snagged their flag. She stuffed it into her swimsuit. In a flash, she was down in the water again, starting the swim back.

"Come on. Come on." Beckett chanted it, as if that could make her faster. She'd already proved her lung capacity was superior, so he didn't worry as much about the long stretch of nothing as he had on the trip over.

They were at the two-and-a-half minute mark when someone on the blue team recognized that their flag had disappeared. On the dock, blue scrambled, trying to figure out whether their flag had straight up flown off the raft in the wind. Then Sarah's head broke the surface of the water fifty feet from shore. The enemy spotted her. Shouts rang out, several people on the raft pointing in her direction.

"Hurry, hurry, hurry!" Beckett began to wave, flailing his arms, urging her to put on some speed.

She paused for only a moment, looking over her shoulder, where three of their kayak jailers were closing the distance. She broke into a smooth butterfly, as she had the day of the swim test, and proved she was still the best swimmer at Camp Firefly Falls. Her hand slapped the muddy bank, and she stumbled out, falling to her knees, gasping. But her eyes were feverish and triumphant as she tugged the sopping wet flag out of her swimsuit and handed it over. "Take it. Get back to base."

Beckett reached out a hand. "Hurry up. Come on."

She shook her head. "I can't move fast enough. I just used all of my energy. Go." The blue team was getting closer to shore. "Go!"

"I'll come back for you!" With one last look at her, Beckett turned and bolted into the trees.

She'd been right about their advantage in this competition. He'd spent more time in these woods than most anyone else, and he knew the quickest way from here to home base—for all the good it did him. They were surrounded. There was no way he'd be able to get to the ladder to go straight up. He'd have to go through the trees.

Good thing we planned for this.

Beckett backtracked to one of the other stations further up the zipline chain. The harness and helmet he'd hidden in the brush for just this situation were still there. He donned them both, and scurried up to the platform, clicking himself onto the zip line and leaping. The wind in his hair was exhilarating, and under other circumstances he'd have whooped with joy. But he didn't want anyone to know he was coming.

He made it from one platform to the next, clipping on, clipping off, clipping on, clipping off, until he was almost all the way back to home base. Someone from below spotted him. "Up there!"

Just one more stretch to go.

Clipping onto the last line, he bellowed, "Incoming!"

His team gave way as he came in hot, going a whole lot faster than he probably should have. Grinning ear to ear, he slammed into the padded center post and handed off the blue flag to a teammate to attach it next to their own where it flapped limply in the breeze.

Someone must have radioed back to home base to make the announcement because the airhorn sounded again and Heather came over the camp loudspeaker announcing, "The red team is the winner!"

And with Sarah's help, they'd done it in less than an hour.

9

It was their last night together. The thrill of this morning's victory had long since faded. What did their success matter when she'd be leaving tomorrow? With that dark cloud looming over them, Sarah struggled to maintain a positive attitude as she trailed Beckett through the trees for the night hike he'd proposed so they could get some privacy. She had no idea where he was taking her, but she was content to follow him anywhere. At least in this.

They'd agreed they didn't want this thing between them to end. Now it was time to talk logistics about how a long-distance relationship would actually work. She was a planner, through and through. It was how she'd succeeded at everything she'd ever set out to do. Making this relationship work would be no different. She was determined.

But she needed those details.

By now, they were far enough from camp proper that she didn't think there'd be anyone around to overhear. Time to address the elephant in the room.

"So, I'd say we have a few things to figure out."

Beckett dropped back, so he could walk beside her instead of in the lead. His strong fingers laced with hers, a grounding touch she needed. "We're going to figure this out. Where do you want to start?"

"Well, the reality is that I won't be here after tomorrow. I'm supposed to meet Taryn in Briarsted to make the swap. I don't actually know how I'm getting back to New York since she couldn't be bothered to let me know the specifics of when she'll be arriving. I might have one more night. I don't know. It will depend on what time she gets in whether or not I'll be able to book a train."

Beckett was silent for a moment. "I guess we can't very well sneak you back to camp with her here. And I don't know that I'll be able to get away tomorrow night. But maybe I can work something out. Just so that we can have another night."

This was the game they been playing for days

Coming up with crazy plans and bargaining chips to buy them just a little more time.

Sarah sighed. "It's going to suck only seeing each other every few weeks."

"Especially with the shit Wi-Fi and reception up here. That'll make it harder to talk."

Ugh. She hadn't thought of that.

"I guess we can go old school and write letters. That might be romantic in some aspects."

"An epistolary romance is not exactly my idea of a good time. But speaking of writing, you can do that anywhere. What if you found somewhere to lease in Briarsted? Maybe found a part-time job while you finish up your thesis? I mean something at camp is obviously out of the question, because that would clearly expose this whole charade."

By this point, Sarah had plenty of concerns on that they'd get exposed anyway. It was one thing when she'd been standing in and no one knew her. But they'd had time to get to know her some, and she hadn't put as much effort into being her sister she intended. Mostly because of Beckett. But she didn't bring that up.

She forced herself to consider what he was suggesting, not just leaping at it because it meant she'd get to see him more often. "I can certainly look, but I don't think I'd be able to find a job that would pay enough to cover renting a place without finding a sublet for my apartment in Brooklyn. And that would be a whole thing. It just makes the most financial sense for me to go back for the rest of the summer, and then take the train out of the city depending on how much time you can get off."

He was quiet for a minute, considering. "I guess it makes the most sense for me to come to you. In the name of keeping your sister's cover. Seems like that would end up probably costing less than renting a place every time you're able to come up. Plus, with my 4-Runner, we won't be dependent on the train schedule."

Sarah didn't love the idea of not getting out of the city again, but she'd do what she had to do. He was right on both counts.

"Speaking of Taryn's cover, there's something else we need to decide. Are we going to have to stage some kind of a fight before I leave to give a reason for why your'e not going to be all lovey-dovey with Taryn? After that whole thing with Diego at breakfast the other day, people are clearly noticing."

"If it comes to that, Taryn and I can stage it later. Right now, I want to spend the last of my time on you."

She tipped her head to his shoulder as they walked. "I am fully in support of that plan. Where are we going anyway?"

"It's a surprise. I wanted to do something special for our last night here."

What had he even had time to come up with given how busy they'd been with work the past few days?

"How much farther?"

"Not too much longer."

The sun had almost fully set by the time she heard the dull roar. Only the faintest orange glow remained in the sky. Fireflies had begun winking in the depths of the trees. It made her think of a fairyland. As if Oberon himself was going to stride out of the trees with an invitation into Otherworld.

She laughed at herself. That kind of romantic thought would make people think she'd been an English major instead of a scientist. Still, she lifted her camera to grab a few shots. They might not turn out, but if they did, they'd be stunning.

The roar got louder the more they walked, and she'd figured it out, even before they broke free of the trees to the edge of the lake.

"Firefly Falls."

Beckett shrugged off his pack. "The one and only."

Sarah kept going, taking in the scene with wonder. It was beautiful. The falls ended in a wide pool that was embraced by arms of rock on both sides. Only the smallest gap—a couple of strides wide—allowed the water to keep flowing on into Lake Waawaatesi beyond. Thick trees wrapped around all sides, giving a remarkable sense of privacy. Stars winked above them, a celestial accent for the light show still happening down here.

Beckett cupped her shoulders from behind, skimming his hands down her arms to link with hers. She automatically leaned back against him, enjoying the feel as he wrapped his arms around her, holding her tight. "You had to see this before you left."

"You didn't tell me to bring a swimsuit."

His mouth dropped to her shoulder, nibbling a line along the column of her throat. "No, I didn't. "

Her body was already beginning to stir. "Do you have ideas, Mr. Hayes?"

His big palm skated down the flat of her belly lingering just above the apex of her thighs. "Absolutely."

Sarah wished—she really, really wished—that she was able to turn off the analytic part of her brain to simply enjoy this beautiful gift he was trying to give her. But that simply wasn't how she operated. "Condoms don't really work in the water."

Unperturbed, Beckett shifted her hair aside and continued the exploration of her nape with his mouth. "No. But there's plenty of other pleasure to be had without them. And I brought blankets for after."

Going skinny-dipping? Making love outdoors, where theoretically anyone could come upon them? It was entirely out of character. The sort of crazy thing her sister would leap at. But maybe this trip was teaching her to embrace that side just a little bit more.

She turned in Beckett's arms, snaking her own around his neck. "I do appreciate a man who can plan." She paused and swallowed. "For the record, I'm on birth control."

Beckett stilled and lifted his head. She couldn't fully see the intensity of his gaze as he stared down at her, but she felt it. "I haven't been with anyone since my ex, and that's been months. I'm clean."

Sarah rose to her toes, bringing them chest to chest, mouth to mouth. "Okay then. Let's make the most of this."

And for the next several hours, that's exactly what they did.

"I did not anticipate that I'd need to utilize *Mission Impossible* tactics to get my stuff out of here unseen."

Beckett couldn't even smile at Sarah's joke. Not today. Not when they were on their way to meet her sister for the official swap. Not when she was leaving.

Instead, he scanned their surroundings, checking to make sure no one else was around the staff parking lot before urging her forward, toward his 4-Runner, which he'd moved as close to the treeline as possible last night. "Go, go, go."

They broke cover, hustling to open the doors and toss her bags into the backseat. Less than a minute later, he was pulling out of the parking lot and onto the long, winding gravel road that led down from Camp Firefly Falls to the highway that would take them past Boone's and on into Briarsted.

From the passenger seat, Sarah watched her phone instead of the scenery. "Surely, once we get to better service, I'll get the message about where and when we're actually supposed to meet, right?"

She'd been asking variants of the same question for the last two days, having expected a text or email with details about her sister's flight and a firmer plan for the switch. But there'd been nothing. Beckett had watched exasperation morph to frustration at the lack of word from Taryn. But now there was a tinge of worry underneath the tone.

Was this a matter of Taryn being thoughtless toward her sister, or had something happened? Beckett didn't know, and he was frustrated on Sarah's behalf, because he could see how this was affecting her.

Reaching over, he squeezed her leg. "Once we hit the highway, the signal's better. You can try calling her again."

And Taryn damned well better answer.

They were both wound up. Today was the end of things. Well, no. Not the end of them. But the end of their everyday. At least for a while. She was due in her thesis advisor's office next week. In New York. Where that advisor expected her back in the lab.

Long distance had been his idea. It was the only plan he'd been able to come up with that would keep Sarah in his life while she figured out what she wanted to. While they *both* figured out what they wanted to do. He'd take whatever weekends or days off with her he could get. In New

York. At camp. Wherever they could manage in between.

It wouldn't be enough for him. Not when he'd gotten used to seeing that blissed out look she got at that first hit of coffee in the morning or the utter hero worship in her eyes when he was the one who provided it. Not when he'd be spending the rest of the summer working alongside a woman who would inevitably remind him of her at every turn but not *be* her.

Damn, that was going to suck.

They were almost to Boone's by the time she made the call. "Hey, it's me. I'm on my way to Briarsted to meet you. Call me back." She hung up. "Straight to voicemail."

"Well, camp's not the only place with lousy reception up here. Maybe she's on her way."

"Hopefully." But the lip Sarah caught between her teeth said she wasn't sure she believed that.

Beckett linked his fingers with hers over the console.

They didn't talk on the rest of the drive. What was there to say? Neither of them was into idle chitchat, and the last thing they wanted to discuss was what was coming. Taryn didn't answer any of the other calls Sarah made on the way to town.

As he turned onto the main street of town, she

blew out a breath. "I don't even know what to look for. She was supposed to be flying out here, not driving. I have no clue if she even thought to reserve a rental car or considered how she was getting here. As it is, I'll have to book a train back down to New York. Chances are, I won't make it on one today, which leaves the question of where the hell I'm staying tonight."

Beckett wanted her back in his bed. But that was hardly practical under the circumstances. "Let's get out and walk a bit. Stretch our legs and see what there is to see."

Sunlight filtered through the lush canopy of oak and maple trees that lined both sides of the street. They strode down the sidewalk, past the red brick and white wooden historic buildings housing boutiques and restaurants and art galleries. Scents of grilled meat and flowers tickled Beckett's nose, reminding him that they'd missed lunch for this trip. It was cute, quaint little town that begged exploration. But he didn't think Sarah saw a bit of it.

When they reached the end of the street, she stopped. "She's not here."

"You don't know that. She could be here somewhere." Though Beckett had his doubts.

She just looked at him. "She's not here. I know."

"Is that one of those twin things?"

"Twinsense. Past experience. I just know that this is not like her." Frustration fully made way for worry now. "I should have heard from her before now. At the very least, as soon as she booked her flights, she should've forwarded them to me. What if something happened to her?"

After all his years as a park ranger, Beckett knew well enough that even experienced outdoorsmen could get into trouble in the wild. He didn't give voice to any of the potential scenarios that immediately popped into his head, instead going into problem-solving mode to keep Sarah calm.

"That seems like something we can find out. Do you have a way to contact the company she worked for? To find out if she really has gotten back from this guide trip?"

"You're right. Let me think. I don't know the number directly, but I think I can find it." She hunched over her phone, fingers flying as she searched for the company's website. "Ah ha!"

Beckett surreptitiously crossed his fingers as she dialed the number.

"Wind River Adventures. This is Roxanne."

"Hi Roxanne. I'm hoping you can help me."

He listened as she explained who she was and that her sister was a guide for their company and she was hoping she could speak to someone who could tell her where Taryn was.

"Of course, I'll wait."

A male voice came on the line, much quieter than the first woman.

"Yes, I'm Sarah Meadows, Taryn's sister. I'm trying to find out if she returned from the last guide trip she took. I was expecting to hear from her by now." Pause. "She hasn't?" Sarah's hand shot out to grab his, and Beckett held on tight. "Well, has she checked in? Do you know whether she's okay? How do you know something didn't go wrong on the trail?" Another pause. "Uh huh. Uh huh."

Sarah sucked in a slow, controlled breath. "I see. Thank you for letting me know. As soon as she returns please tell her to contact me immediately. It's important."

The moment she hung up the phone, she dropped her head to his chest. Her voice was slightly muffled against his shirt. "Apparently they radioed in from the trail asking for an extension. She did evidently ask that her boss contact me, but they got my number wrong and just... didn't try to reach back out to correct it. They expect her in tomorrow."

Beckett stroked a hand down her hair. "So she's not going to make it back in time for the certification tests." It wasn't a question. There was no way she'd be getting back from the trail at some point tomorrow and be able to find flights back east in time to make it all the way to camp first thing in the morning the day after.

Sarah shook her head.

I don't have to say goodbye yet. The relief that crashed through him at that was enormous, but he didn't share it.

Sarah straightened, pinching the bridge of her nose. Every line of her body shouted anger and frustration and exhaustion. And above the rest of it, resignation because this was so clearly par for the course for how things worked with her sister.

"Well, that's..." He trailed off, trying to find some word to describe the situation that wouldn't be offensive to her sister.

"That's Taryn. This has been her all our lives. I love her, but half the time, I think she needs a damned keeper."

And now Beckett understood her perfectionism and insistence on finishing things as he watched the relaxation and freedom Sarah had achieved over the past few days melt away.

"At least she did try to get a message to me, even if it didn't work. That was something. But what are we going to do?"

He was going to hang on to every last second with her.

That wasn't what she was asking, though. "Well, you're going to take the certification tests. You've flown through all the training and everything I've thrown at you. There is nothing that they're going to put you through on a test that you can't handle." He tightened his hold on her. "And, on the plus side, we're going to embrace the fact that we get a little more time together."

Sarah cuddled closer, one corner of her mouth lifting. "Silver lining, huh?"

He smiled back, brushing his lips to hers. "The brightest."

10

I'm so sorry. I'm on my way.

Taryn's apology text had come in overnight. Sarah hadn't replied. What was there to say? She'd known there was no possible way her sister would make it for the certification. And she hadn't.

Frustration and anger were likewise pointless. They wouldn't change anything, and would only serve as a distraction Sarah couldn't afford. She had enough of that already in the form of more texts from Dr. Osborne reiterating how badly she was needed back in the lab, with a heavy implication that her acquiescence would impact her standing in the program. Or maybe Sarah was just reading that into the messages because of her own anxiety. But that was for the day after tomorrow, when she was back in the city.

Her only priority right now was to pass these tests to the best of her ability.

And she had.

Over the course of the morning, they'd knocked out the written test and passed everyone through final First Aid and CPR certification. As soon as lunch was through, staff would be breaking off into smaller groups for individual activity certification with the outside instructors who'd been brought in for that purpose.

Though her stomach was twisted into knots, Sarah nibbled at her sandwich, knowing she needed fuel for this last leg of certification day. Objectively, she knew she was ready. Beckett had made sure of it, and she trusted him. But she couldn't shake the sick sense in her stomach that something would go horribly wrong.

Up on the dais, Heather clapped her hands. "Okay, people! Let's get this show on the road."

No way around it. Even if Taryn miraculously appeared, there was no easy way to swap out with her, so Sarah was doing this.

Tossing the remains of her lunch, she joined Beckett, the certification instructor, and the rest of the climbing staff for the walk out to the equipment shed. When Heather and Michael fell into step with the group, that clench in her gut got worse. She wished desperately for a private few minutes with Beckett, so he could hug her and reiterate that she had this. But they were keeping things strictly professional today.

It's fine. Everything's going to be fine.

The certifying instructor, Richard, brought them inside one at a time, where they were asked to demonstrate knowledge of equipment. When her turn came, Sarah rolled through it as if she'd been doing it for years, reciting everything Beckett had taught her, with only the barest of hesitations when her brain decided to remind her of all the up-close-and-personal study sessions they'd had in here. Afterward, they trooped en masse to Boulder Mountain for the practical demonstration. As he was already certified for far more challenging climbs than this, Beckett would be positioned up top to observe and intervene as necessary.

Before he made the climb, he paused just long enough to brush the back of her hand with his. Grounding her.

I can do this.

When her turn rolled around, Sarah started on lead, working seamlessly with Diego as he took the intermediate path up for his own top rope test. Once Diego was back on the ground, they swapped. The whole process went smoothly, and Sarah shot Beckett a grin as she reached the top.

"Nearly done," he murmured. "You're doing great."

"I'm just ready for this to be over."

They took the descent together.

"Now, for our last test of the day, each of you will be expected to demonstrate the ability to properly and immediately catch at least three simulated falls," Richard announced. "Beckett has volunteered to be our test dummy. Now who's first?"

"Me." Sarah stepped up immediately. This was the last piece that stood between her and being finished.

They went through the safety check and clipped in.

"Belay on?" he asked.

"On belay."

"Climbing."

"Climb on."

Beckett took the ascent fast, mimicking some of the rookie mistakes they were bound to encounter with campers over the summer. She knew he could handle it, knew he was doing this on purpose, both for the test and so she'd be done. But it didn't stop her heart from leaping into her throat each time he slipped. She took the first two falls like a champ, stopping his descent exactly as she should. Then Beckett headed on up to the top for the long drop. At the apex, he glanced down toward the crowd, then beyond them.

Gaze focused on him, Sarah saw the shock an instant before his muttered, "Oh sh—"

Then he was falling. A real fall, not one of the simulations this time. For one endless second, fear stopped Sarah's heart. Then she threw herself into action, braking his descent as she'd been taught. "Gotcha!"

His momentum and greater weight hauled her several feet up the rock face. But she'd caught him.

"You okay?" she called.

"Yep." But there was something in his face that said he wasn't.

"Holy shit!" Diego exclaimed. "There are two of them!"

Dangling against the rock, Sarah just closed her eyes. Because she knew, even without looking.

"Ready to lower." Beckett's soft voice kicked her back into action.

After a brief hesitation, she managed, "Lowering."

For the couple of minutes it took to get both of

them on the ground again, Sarah kept her blinders on. She didn't look. Didn't break character or protocol.

At the base of Boulder Mountain, she and Beckett unclipped from the ropes. And there was no more avoiding the elephant she knew was standing behind her. Sucking in a breath, she turned to face her sister.

Taryn's thumbs were tucked in the pockets of her khaki shorts. Her dark blonde hair was pulled back in a braid. Her skin was more tan than Sarah's, and she'd lost weight since they'd last seen each other. In that moment, Sarah realized the utter idiocy of their plan. Yes, they were identical twins, but right now they wouldn't fool anyone who knew them. And Sarah had been around the rest of the Camp Firefly Falls staff long enough that, of the two of them, they knew her.

The Tullys and everyone else were staring, gazes bouncing back and forth, as if not trusting their own eyes.

"So you're a twin?" Diego asked. "Seems like that's something you might've mentioned."

But Sarah was focused on the camp owners, trying to gauge their reaction. Shock. Confusion. They hadn't yet clued in to what this likely meant.

Heather was the first to find her voice. "What...?"

For once, Sarah stayed quiet. This had been her sister's plan. It was on her to make explanations.

"Right," Taryn said. "This conversation would probably best be had in an office somewhere."

"Oh, I think I saw this movie," Laura muttered. "One of them is either hiding from a prince fiancé or is secretly an international spy."

If only.

Michael's usually affable face shifted from shock into something that was a mix of dread and the start of what was probably anger. Without a word, he gestured toward the trail back to the main lodge.

Time for all of them to face the music.

THIS IS where it all falls apart.

Sarah didn't know what she'd thought would happen. Maybe for Taryn to just impersonate her until such a time as they could make the switch properly. But she'd walked right up and asked to speak privately before the Tullys could make the request themselves. And maybe that was good.

She was clearly intent on taking responsibility for herself, which was progress. But how were they going to explain Sarah's presence here? And what was going to be the fallout for her for participating in this charade?

Taryn interrupted her train of thought. "That was a nice catch back there."

In the seconds it had taken to do her job, she'd lost five years off her life seeing Beckett plummet like that.

"Didn't know you knew how to do that," Taryn added.

"I've had a good teacher. And anyway, it shouldn't have been me. Where the hell have you been?" Sarah hissed. "And how are you even here? Danny said you weren't getting back from the trail until yesterday."

Taryn shot her an assessing look, clearly wondering who that teacher had been, but she answered the question. "My client wanted to extend the trip for a sum I couldn't refuse. But when he found out the pickle I was in with this job, he flew me out on his private jet last night. I really thought I'd make it this morning, but there was an issue with my reservation at the car rental place, and construction on the route from the airport, and... Well. I'm sorry. I got here as soon as I could."

Private jet?

Sarah couldn't even respond to that. "Yeah, well, I'm thinking it's too little, too late, now."

In the moment, she couldn't even care that more money from this mystery client meant more of the debt paid off. All she could focus on was the deep sense of failure and dread at what was coming. Her time here was well and truly over now. No more borrowed moments or reprieves.

"It'll be okay," Taryn soothed.

Sarah doubted it.

Michael shut the door to the office. "Okay, I think I'm well within my rights to ask what the hell is going on?"

"There's a very simple explanation for this," Taryn began.

Heather crossed her arms. "I'd love to hear it since this is clearly not simply a case of one sister coming to visit the other."

"I'm Taryn Meadows. The actual Taryn Meadows you hired. This is my sister, Sarah, who's been impersonating me the last two weeks."

The Tullys stared, giving them both the hairy eyeball even as they shared a fresh round of dumbfounded shock at the resemblance. Sarah shifted, wishing she could just sink through the floor. This sounded even worse than when she'd told Beckett. She braced herself for a curt, "Get out."

Eventually, Michael asked, "Why?"

"Because I was stuck out in Wyoming on my previous job past when I thought I'd be finished, and I was going to miss orientation. So I asked her to fill in for me."

Heather narrowed her eyes. "And you were, what? Going to just swap out after the fact without telling anybody?"

"That was the original plan, yes. I was supposed to be back to take all the certification tests myself, but I ran into travel difficulties."

Michael frowned. "And you're coming clean now, why?"

Taryn hesitated only a moment before lifting her chin. "Because it's the right thing to do. I should never have asked Sarah to step in for me. I should've come to you directly when the problem arose, even if it meant losing the job. And I realize I'm probably losing it anyway, but at least my conscience will be clear."

A part of Sarah wanted to cheer that her sister was taking responsibility. It was the adult thing to do. But did she have to do it like this? Because the likelihood that Sarah would be welcome here ever again was virtually nil. When Michael and

Heather turned matching expressions of betrayal on her, Sarah's last shred of hope that she might be able to ask them for a job for herself died a swift death.

She hunched her shoulders. "I'm sorry for the deception. I was just trying to do her a favor."

Heather pinched the bridge of her nose. "I should have had more coffee this morning."

"You and me both," Sarah muttered. No one said anything for several moments, and abruptly she wanted out. Away from this situation. From her sister. Anywhere she could actually breathe through the panic that was trying to claw its way out of her chest. "Unless there's anything else?" She started toward the door. "I understand you're upset and would like me gone. My bag is already packed. I'll get off the premises immediately."

If she was lucky, maybe she'd get a chance to say goodbye to Beckett.

Before she could cross the room, a brisk knock sounded, and the door swung open without invitation. Beckett barged in. "Don't make any rash decisions."

Presumably he was speaking to the Tullys, but his eyes zeroed straight in on her. She read so much in that gaze. Temper. Concern. Reassurance that she wasn't in this alone.

"Yes, Beck, please join the discussion," Michael said drily.

"Sorry. But I have something to say."

The determined glint in his eyes had Sarah stepping toward him. "Beckett, don't."

The last thing she wanted was him going to bat for her and losing *his* job.

He just shot her an *I've got this* wave. "I know this is a weird situation, but I didn't want y'all tossing anybody out without listening. This isn't on Sarah."

Heather went brows up. "Wait, you knew she wasn't Taryn?"

"I figured it out pretty fast."

"And you chose *not* to turn her in," Michael confirmed.

"I did." Beckett's jaw firmed, his shoulders squaring. "You're the one who kept spouting off about Pinecone Lodge."

Huh?

Whatever that was about clearly meant something to the Tullys. Michael swore and Heather straightened, coming to very focused attention.

"Please don't take anything out on Beckett," Sarah insisted. "None of this was his idea."

That chiseled jaw turned to granite. Stubborn through and through. "Training you was my idea.

And I stand by it. You can do the job. You just proved that."

"By rights we should fire the lot of you," Michael said. "This whole thing could have been an insurance nightmare."

"Nobody got hurt," Beckett insisted. "And Sarah passed all the certifications."

"Not the point. The job wasn't hers."

"Michael," Heather chided. "We can't afford to lose any senior staff. Not at this point. Beckett, you're not going anywhere."

Something in Sarah unclenched. At least he still had his job. That was so much more than she'd feared. But where did that leave the rest of them?

"As for Taryn—the real one—" Heather shifted her gaze and shook her head. "I wish you'd come to us before. We might have been able to come to an agreement, but under the circumstances, as you weren't here for any of the training or the certification tests, we can't hire you."

Sarah had known that was coming and still the news felt like a blow. Maybe because of the sheer inevitability finally collapsing on her head.

Taryn's throat worked, but she merely nodded. "Understood."

"What about Sarah?" Beckett demanded.

"What about her? She's not in any kind of trouble." Heather waved a hand in her direction. "What would we charge her with? Conspiracy to do a good job? She aced everything."

"Of course, she did." Taryn softened the remark with a grin that Sarah couldn't return.

Heather sat back against the desk. "Look, we don't appreciate the lie, but you did an amazing job while you were here. So don't feel like you have to slink off like some kind of criminal."

That was something, at least. Swallowing hard against the knot in her throat, Sarah murmured, "Thank you."

"What is it you actually do?" Michael asked.

"I'm in graduate school at Columbia. Neuropsychology." Somehow, making that announcement didn't bring her the sense of achievement it always had before.

"Huh." Whatever he'd expected, that clearly wasn't it. "Well, all right then."

Beckett's hand snaked out to tangle with hers, and it took everything she had not to turn into him and bury her face against his chest.

Michael shot a measured look at their joined hands. "I'm guessing you two have some things to talk about before you go."

"Do you need me tonight?" Beckett asked.

Heather's face softened. "We'll manage. But you'll be on deck in the morning."

"Understood. Thank you."

"I guess you're all dismissed," Michael announced. "We need to get back to the others."

"Yes, sir." Taryn turned back. "I apologize again for... well, all of this."

Sarah didn't stick around to see what reaction either of the Tullys had to this assertion. All of it was too little, too late. She strode out of the office, Beckett tight on her heels.

"Sarah, wait up."

Taryn's voice followed her down the hall. The last thing Sarah wanted was to talk with her twin about any of this. Not when she was feeling so raw.

"Look, I know you're mad—"

Sarah spun, lifting the hand not clasped in Beckett's. "No. You're on my shit list right now. I'm not spending what little time I have left here arguing or listening to your excuses."

Stunned pain flashed across Taryn's face. "But Sarah—"

"I'm done, T." With so much more than her sister could know. "Let's go, Beckett."

11

Beckett woke reaching for Sarah and found only an empty stretch of bed. At the coolness of the sheets, he opened his eyes. The room was dark and quiet. For a moment, he wondered if she had simply sneaked out the night. Then he spotted her perched on the window seat, arms wrapped around her up-drawn knees as she stared out into the dark. Not quite so dark now. Her body was a silhouette against the gradually lightning sky. Dawn wouldn't be too far off. And with it, the goodbye that neither of them wanted to face.

He sat up. "You okay?" He felt stupid asking the question. Neither of them was okay right now. But he needed to know what had kept her from sleep. Other than their own insatiable need to fill their last hours together with as much of each other as they could manage.

"I didn't mean to wake you." Her voice held that quiet, pre-coffee rasp but no sign of grogginess. She was definitely awake.

"You didn't. Come back to bed." He patted the mattress beside him.

There wouldn't be time for much in the way of sleep, and he didn't think either of them would rest easy at this point. Not with her departure so imminent. But he wanted no distance between them before there had to be.

Sarah slid off the window seat and padded across the room to slip beneath the covers. The sheets whispered as she slid over to wrap around him. Her bare skin was cool to the touch.

Beckett tucked around her. "You're freezing. How long have you been up?"

Her shoulders twitched in a shrug. "I don't know. A while. I couldn't sleep. My head's too full."

After they'd left the main lodge yesterday, she'd stuck to what she'd said. There'd been no talk of her sister or the situation. He'd packed an overnight bag, and they'd gathered her things, loading them into his SUV and driving into Briarsted. On that drive she'd seemingly compartmentalized the whole thing, such that they'd spent the afternoon strolling like any tourist couple, enjoying a fine meal at one of the local restaurants before settling in for the night at a B&Bs in the foothills. They hadn't spoken of today. Not of the practicalities or worries of the future. But Beckett could feel all of them in the tension thrumming in her body.

Tipping his head, he pressed his lips to her bare shoulder. "Are we gonna talk about it now?"

"What good is talking about going to do? It doesn't change anything. I'm still leaving in a matter of hours."

Her words held too much of a tone of goodbye. So had the desperate way she'd turned to him in the night. He'd told himself that it was simply soaking up every last bit of contact they could, but now he wondered if something more significant had changed. The moment her sister had arrived, Sarah had thrown up walls against everyone. Him included. In a sense, she was with him, but she wasn't *with* him.

Knowing he couldn't let this lie, he stroked a hand down the length of her back, wanting to soothe, even as he knew he was about to destroy their last little hint of peace. "Have you heard from Taryn?"

"Yeah. She's freaking out about what happens next. I've been letting her stew in it for a bit."

"You have to talk to her at some point."

Sarah's chest rose and fell against his with a bone-deep sigh. "I know. I've got to help her figure out how to get out of this latest hole she's dug."

That wasn't at all what he'd meant. Beckett chose his words carefully. "No, I mean... Her behavior has had a profound impact on your life. You can't keep rescuing her. At some point, she has to stand on her own two feet. That's part of being a grown-ass adult. Beyond which, you deserve the chance to stand on yours."

She lay quiet for a long time. "You're right. You're absolutely right. But that's not today. It's to my benefit to help her logically consider things before she gets some other scheme as crazy as this one was."

Why did that sting so much? It wasn't as if she was choosing to leave him today because of her sister. Not really. She had obligations back in New York. But it still felt as if she were choosing everything else over him. Especially when he knew down to his marrow that going back to Columbia wasn't going to make her happy.

"Are you having second thoughts?" The words slipped out unbidden.

"Second thoughts about what?"

"Us. The long distance thing." *Whether I can make you happy.*

They'd agreed to this. Discussed all the logistics and how they'd make it work. She'd been on board. But Beckett couldn't shake the sense that something fundamental had shifted yesterday. He'd watched her shift into someone else the moment her twin had arrived. So he braced himself for her answer.

Sarah pressed a soft kiss over his heart. "No. I haven't changed my mind." She sighed. "I mean, it's going to suck. I don't know when I'll get to see you again."

He had a partial answer to that, at least. "Well, sooner rather than later. Thanks to you. Red team is first up for choosing days off, remember?"

He'd hoped that reminding her of that victory would lighten the mood a little. But it didn't.

She sighed again, settling her head back in the curve of his shoulder that seemed made just for her. "It won't be the same."

It definitely wouldn't. Nothing could compare to working side-by-side with her. Seeing her over breakfast. Having her in his bed. But if his life had taught him anything, it was patience.

"Maybe not, but in the grand scheme of things,

summer isn't that long. The last session is over at the end of August. Even if circumstances prevented us from managing to see each other until then—and I'll move heaven and hell to make sure that we do—it's only a few months. It's a pause, not an ending. We aren't over." He hesitated, then gave voice to his biggest fear. "Unless you want it to be."

Her arms tightened around him in a possessive hold. "No. I meant what I said. I haven't changed my mind. I don't want this to end. But I'd be lying if I said I wasn't afraid."

"Afraid of what?"

In the ensuing silence, Beckett could hear the soft *woosh woosh* of his own pulse in his ears as he waited for her answer.

"I've been on this path all my life. I've always known where I was going, what I was doing. There has never been a point when I did not have a plan. I'm someone who thinks seventeen steps ahead, anticipating problems and dealing with them before they ever arise. And now I can't even see around the next corner. The idea of that terrifies me. It's one thing to talk about changing my whole life when I'm with you. It's not scary when you're right beside me. But I worry how I'm going to react when I get back to New York, and you're not there to talk me down when I freak out."

Beckett took the time before answering, because he was operating on very little sleep and didn't want to make a misstep. "What exactly are you afraid of? That you'll freak out and finish your thesis and decide to stay in grad school anyway? That you'll up and decide to end things because you can't take the distance? That you walk away from everything with no parachute or net like I did?"

"I don't know. Maybe a little bit of all those things. I just know it doesn't feel good or right. Things are too unsettled. I *need* a plan, and I'm not to get the chance to make one before I leave today."

Beckett resumed the slow stroking of her back. "Life can be scary business. And yeah, that's a lot easier to handle when someone you care about is by your side. But just because I am not right next to you, not close enough to touch, doesn't mean I'm not with you. If you're anxious or upset, all you have to do is reach out. Phone call, text, email, carrier pigeon. Whatever works for you. I'll be there. As soon as I can."

She lapsed into silence again, and he wondered if he'd said the wrong thing.

"Dawn is breaking. We don't have that much more time. You have to get back to camp, to work. I've got to catch a train." She rolled closer to him, finding his mouth with hers. "Be with me one more time. So that I'll still feel you long after I'm back home."

With the sun already peeking through the curtains, how could he do anything but what she asked?

SARAH GOT BACK to her apartment by noon, dropping her bag onto the floor with a thump. For a long moment, she just stared at the little box she'd called home for the past three years. After the luxury of Camp Firefly Falls, all she could see was the dinginess of the used furniture she'd scrounged up and the drab shade of gray on the walls that seemed to close in on her, further exacerbating the sense of claustrophobia she'd been fighting from the moment she'd gotten back to the city. Had it always looked this pathetic? Had she simply been so focused on school that she hadn't even noticed the lack of warmth in what was supposed to be home?

Familiar thumps and groans sounded from the

neighboring apartment. The newlyweds again. Except now they made her remember this morning and her last hour with Beckett before he'd dropped her at the train station. The ache she'd managed to ignore for the better part of the trip back to the city flared bright. God, how could she miss him this much already?

Unable to face unpacking or laundry or shopping for groceries, Sarah shut the door and headed back out to the street in hopes that a walk would help loosen the steel band around her chest.

Hours passed as she wandered, looking for... what? Answers to why she felt so utterly wretched? It wasn't about Beckett. Or at least, it wasn't all about him. They'd more or less sorted the details of the long distance thing. It would suck, as long distance always sucked. But she believed they could survive it. What she wasn't at all certain of any longer was whether she could survive being back here, in this life. It was as if she'd been forced into an ill-fitting hair suit. What had been familiar and normal now felt itchy and wrong. Like someone else's skin.

She'd experienced a different side of herself at camp while she'd been acting, ironically, more like her sister. It was tough to admit there'd been anything positive in that, but had she stuck purely to her own stubborn path, she never would've met Beckett. But was she so changed by the experience that she truly couldn't come back? Or was this simply an epic case of post-vacation blues because she hadn't taken true time off in longer than she could remember?

Exhausted and no closer to any sort of answer, Sarah dragged herself back to her apartment. The music spilling from behind her closed door had her bracing, not out of fear but of temper. She knew that playlist. She let herself inside and found Taryn stretched out on the corduroy sofa, bare feet twitching to Tracy Chapman, completely at home in a space that wasn't even hers. When Sarah had given her a key years ago, she hadn't truly expected her to use it.

Taryn took one look at her and swiveled her feet to the floor, stopping the music mid chorus. "You're still mad."

Suddenly all the frustration, all the angst she'd been wrestling came boiling out. "Of course I'm still mad! Yet again, you have disrupted my perfectly ordered life with all your chaos and irresponsibility. Not only didn't I get a single word written on my thesis while I was up there, I met the perfect guy. And then I had to leave him to come back here because you ruined any chance that I might be able to make something work up there because you couldn't even follow through on your own lunatic plan. Which, by the way, would never have worked. Not to mention I was fucking terrified when I didn't hear from you when I was supposed to. I don't *want* this."

"Want what, exactly?"

"This stress. These incompatible wants. My life was *fine* before I put it on hold to help you out—again—and now I don't know if I can go back to it!"

Taryn's brows arched toward her hairline. "First off, I'm sorry I worried you. Truly. I had no idea my boss hadn't notified you like I asked. Second, was your life really fine if you don't want to go back to it?"

Because that was too close to the question she'd been asking herself all afternoon, Sarah just glared at her twin.

"I saw how you looked at Beckett. More, I saw how he looked at you. I think you need to do something you've never done in your life."

Still riding on temper, Sarah couldn't quite hold back the sarcastic sneer. "And what's that?"

"I think you should quit."

The mere suggestion of it had her back going up. "Excuse me?"

"All our lives, you've put the expectations and happiness of everyone else ahead of you. You've stuck out a million and one things you don't actually like, that don't make you happy or fill you with joy or purpose, because you didn't want to upset someone. When are you going to realize that *you* are the one who matters most in your life? I know you think I'm irresponsible and flighty, and no question, I've made some dumb decisions. But it's led me to a life I honestly love. And maybe it doesn't have the degree of stability that you'd prefer, or the prestige to satisfy that sense of competition, but it's mine.

"It's more than obvious that you care for Beckett. You want time with him... then make that time. Take a risk on him. If it doesn't work out, school will still be there on the other side. With your credentials, there's no way they won't let you back in. But what if it does work out? What if he's your perfect match, and you're prioritizing a degree you're apathetic about in a city you've grown to hate to appease... who? Give yourself permission to fail and not have all the answers for once. Sometimes the right answer is one you'd never have considered at all."

It so much echoed what Beckett had been trying to tell her, but somehow it was harder coming from her sister, and that just pissed Sarah off. It was so easy for Taryn to say "Just quit." It wasn't her life. But Sarah couldn't deny she'd made some good points.

Taryn rose to her feet and moved toward the athletic sandals she'd kicked off. "Look, I went back to talk to the Tullys before I left."

Sarah frowned, wondering where she was going with this. "Did you sweet talk them into hiring you anyway?" That was pretty much on brand for Taryn. And it usually worked out for her.

"No. I talked them into hiring you."

"What?" She couldn't have heard that right.

"If you want the job, the one that you just did the orientation for, the one that I was supposed to have, it's yours. They're willing to hire you. So the option is on the table for you to do exactly what I think you want to do and spend the summer at Camp Firefly Falls with Beckett, while you figure out what the hell comes next."

Flabbergasted, Sarah could only stare. Taryn had gone out on a limb and made this effort... for her. And she'd pulled it off. The band that had been constricting Sarah's chest since she'd left loosened a little. Because it *was* what she wanted.

Her phone vibrated with a text.

Compulsively, she flipped it over, in case it was Beckett. But it was her thesis advisor.

Dr. Osborne: **Hope you made it safely back. Looking forward to meeting with you tomorrow. Lots of exciting things to discuss!**

Her normal life was calling, and one way or the other, she had to give it an answer.

Taryn scooped up the bags she'd piled in the corner and moved toward the door.

"Where are you going?"

Her twin flashed a smile. "I don't know. I haven't decided yet. But it's long past time for me to manage my own life and stop depending on you to help me fix my mistakes. You need to be more like me right now, and I need to be more like you."

Crossing the room, she wrapped Sarah in a hug. "I love you, sis. And I've not said it enough that I appreciate everything you've done to help save me from myself all these years."

With one last squeeze, she was gone, leaving Sarah alone with her thoughts.

12

Beckett: **Good luck with your meeting today.**

Sarah stared at the text, wishing she felt more reassured. But the vibrations of the subway car through the hard plastic seat only served to highlight the vaguely queasy sensation in her stomach. The one she'd had since boarding the train to come back to New York. She'd blamed it on poor sleep. On being heart-sick and missing Beckett already. On the feeling of total claustrophobia she'd had from the moment she'd stepped back onto city streets, with their wall-to-wall people. She'd thought of everything her sister had said well into the wee hours, and she still hadn't made up her mind. It didn't seem fair to even mention it to Beckett until she had.

Pocketing her phone without answering, she struggled to get herself into the right headspace for this meeting. The whole reason she'd taken time off this summer had been to finish her thesis. Dr. Osborne would be expecting progress. She had so little of that to show for the past weeks, and she didn't have a good reason why. Nothing had occurred to her by the time the train came to a stop at her destination.

Sarah rose with several other passengers, weaving her way around all the bodies, getting jostled on her way to the platform door. Her chest went tight at the sense of restriction, and she hurried up the stairs to the relative relief of the surface. The summer heat was stifling, bouncing off all the concrete and asphalt to create an oven effect. The noise-canceling earbuds piping Prokofiev into her ears weren't enough to overcome the cacophony of traffic and construction, and the stench of exhaust did nothing to relieve the constriction in her lungs. She did her best to block everything out as she hurried the rest of the way to the building the housed her advisor's office and lab.

At the door to Dr. Osborne's office, she paused

to try and center herself. But the door opened before she could do more than take a breath.

A trim Black woman in her habitual uniform of neat slacks and tailored Oxford cloth shirt, Debra Osborne looked up, her brown eyes magnified by the tortoise shell glasses she wore. "Sarah! Excellent. Come on in. These copies can wait." She backed up and retreated to her desk.

Helpless to do anything else, Sarah followed.

Her butt had barely hit the visitor's chair before Dr. Osborne started in.

"I know you've taken the summer to work on your thesis. How's that going?"

Though she'd anticipated the question, her cheeks flushed hot with frustration and shame. She wasn't accustomed to failure. "Not great. I'm still struggling with writer's block. I've made some progress, but not as much as I'd like." She paused and admitted the truth. "I'm not entirely sure I'm going to be ready to defend in August."

Dr. Osborne merely blinked, unperturbed. "That happens sometimes. But you'll get it done whenever you get it done. Classes start in the fall. You'll get back into the swing of things. And actually, one of the that's one of the things that I really wanted to talk to you about. You're one of the best and brightest graduate students in this department. The funding for that NIH grant came in, and I want you on my team from the ground up."

Sarah blinked, struggling to pull herself out of the tailspin she'd entered into prematurely. It was hugely flattering to be asked to participate in this project. The research experience alone would look amazing on her vitae. Hell, all the research experience she'd gained working with this woman had been incredible from both a professional and academic standpoint. She ought to be preening at this kind of praise and opportunity. This was exactly what she'd been working for in this program.

And yet... she couldn't muster any enthusiasm at all for the project.

Her advisor was still talking. "—the project is hitting the ground running basically immediately, so if you want to do this, you'd need to start ASAP. I know you were planning on finishing your thesis, but you said yourself that's not going well. I need you back in the lab to start practically yesterday, so we can get things rolling."

Instead of any sense of excitement or rightness, Sarah felt a cage door clanging shut.

She thought of Beckett. Of everything she'd been reconsidering the past two weeks about her life and what came next. If she said yes to this, the next several years of her life would be consumed with finishing the damned thesis that she didn't want to look at anymore, on top of spearheading her own research for an even longer dissertation. It would mean staying trapped in this city, in these halls, for who knew how long. And she just... couldn't see herself doing that anymore.

"It's a huge honor that you'd consider me, and I really appreciate the opportunity, but I'm afraid I have to decline." As soon as the words came out of her mouth, her inner voice began shrieking. *What are you doing? You've worked for years for this! Don't throw it away!*

Dr. Osborne stared, clearly taken aback by her answer. Her gaze focused in fully for the first time. "Are you okay? I mean, is everything okay with you, your family?"

"No." That was the God's honest truth. "I think I need to quit the program."

Concern filled those familiar eyes. "Sarah, if you need to take a leave of absence to deal with whatever this is, we can hold your position in the department. Defer it for a semester or a year."

She could take this. It was what Taryn had suggested. Sort of. A full semester or year off would give her the chance to figure out what she wanted. With a serious break she'd gain clarity. It was really the best option. She opened her mouth to say so.

"I appreciate that. Truly. But I don't think this is the right path for me."

Wait. What?

Her advisor leaned forward. "Sarah, you are one of our most gifted students."

"You're right. I'm very good at school. I've essentially made a career of it. But I can't be a professional student forever. I don't want to teach. I really don't want to do research. I need to do something else with my life."

Admitting it out loud loosened the vise around her chest. Finally.

The older woman's jaw was hanging open as she clearly struggled to wrap her brain around this sudden shift. "What would you do instead?"

"I have no idea." Sarah shoved down her instinctive panic at that. "But this is not going to make me happy. Someone taught me recently that there is more to life than achievement. I sincerely appreciate everything you've done for me, and I'm sorry I won't be able to join you on this project going forward."

She shoved up from her chair and walked out. Her steps quickened on the way to the stairs. By the time she got to the front doors of the building, she burst through as if the hounds of hell were on her heels. She ran full-tilt for several blocks, all the way to the subway station that would get her back to her apartment.

If she was going to blow up the rest of her perfectly ordered life, she had some packing to do.

Beckett officially hated people.

Why the hell had he thought this job was a good idea? Singles Week had been a nightmare, with the air so thick with lust he could practically taste it. Camp was covered in singles out to find a temporary hookup and even a smaller handful hoping to find a real connection. The staff had gotten their Banging Bingo winner—Charlie—by Tuesday. Beckett himself had seen more than one bare ass as he'd inadvertently stumbled upon couples in various compromising positions. He'd taken to making all sorts of noise while walking, just to announce his presence lest he stumble upon any more scenes that required brain bleach.

He wanted to go be a hermit on a mountain. Preferably with Sarah. Except she'd gone incommunicado since she'd gotten back to New York, other than one text to say she'd made it back safely, and that she missed him already.

She had a hell of a way of showing it.

Unable to buckle down his shit mood enough to deal with guests, he managed to hand off his assignments for the next couple of hours. Hiking or climbing would've been preferable to being stuck in his own head, but he couldn't leave campus at this point, so he retreated to the equipment shed. If Michael or Heather came to find him, he'd tell them he was triple checking ropes or something. They'd all already been triple checked, but it was something to do with his hands.

He realized his own miscalculation as he shut himself inside. His gaze unerringly went to the table, and he couldn't help but imagine Sarah there, eyes full of heat. This wasn't going to improve his mood, but at least it was away from prying eyes. Pulling down several coils of rope, he tossed them onto the table and began the process of examining the sheaths all over again.

Why the hell hadn't Sarah responded to his texts or answered his calls? He was 99% sure she was at least physically okay. On more than one occasion, he'd seen the little bubble with three dots pop up, indicating she was composing a response. But she'd sent nothing. Had she gotten back to the city and decided that was the life she wanted after all? Was she just going to quietly ghost him? If the relationship withered that easily, she obviously wasn't the right woman for him. But he just couldn't accept that.

Maybe the meeting with her thesis advisor hadn't gone well and she was quietly falling apart by herself. That seemed like something she'd do. Freak out on her own rather than pull anyone else in for help or comfort.

Sarah had left here with the intention of helping her sister figure out her next moves. That meant she'd seen or talked to her. Probably. Maybe he should try to get in touch with Taryn. Not that he had her contact info, but it would've been in her original hire paperwork. Surely, Michael or Heather would give it to him. She'd at least know for sure whether Sarah was okay. Right?

Beckett hated being in the dark. Hated not knowing what else to do. He needed to talk to her. Maybe he needed to do it in person. Get to the city to confront her directly about what the hell was going on. Figure out what went wrong and how to fix it. If it could be fixed. When was his next day off?

Not soon enough. Not even with the capture

the flag boon his team had won. Which left him up shit creek without a paddle.

The door to the equipment shed opened. Bracing himself to face-off with some random couple looking for a place to hook up, he turned. He couldn't immediately make out more than a person-shape in the doorway. Their features were obscured by the flare of light behind them.

"If you're looking for a place to make out, this is not it."

"Oh, I don't know. I have some pretty fond memories of doing exactly that right over there on that table."

Beckett froze as the door shut, closing him in with Sarah. She wore khaki shorts that bared most of the mile-long length of her tan legs, and a Camp Firefly Falls T-shirt. Her blonde hair was pulled half up, away from her face.

"Hey."

"What? How?" He sputtered. Five whole days she'd said nothing, and now she was here?

Her lips curved in a hesitant smile. "I missed you."

She was *here*. "God, I missed you, too."

Beckett's feet unglued from the floor and he closed the distance between them to pull her into his arms. Her mouth unerringly found his and for the first time in days, he could finally breathe. Wrapping her tight in his arms, he soaked in her scent. "Are you up for the weekend? I didn't know you were coming."

Sarah pulled back to look into his eyes, expression suddenly serious.

Fuck. Was she about to break up with him? Had she come all the way up here to do that face-to-face.

"No, actually." She took a deep breath. "I quit my graduate program."

Honest to God shock rippled through him. "Seriously?"

Her laugh was wry. "Yeah. I've hyperventilated half a dozen times since walking out of my advisor's office. But it's the right choice." Her fingers squeezed his. "Seeing you here now, I know it's the right choice."

"Taryn actually convinced the Tullys to hire me for the summer. So I'm taking her job—the job you trained me for—while I figure out what comes next. Because I choose you, I choose us."

"Sarah." He pressed his brow to hers. "You won't regret it."

"I certainly won't regret you. As to the rest... well, it's scary as hell. But for once, I'm taking a page out of my sister's book. I have no idea how she lives not knowing the next eighty-two steps for what comes next, but I'm trying to learn to be okay with it."

This was everything he hadn't dared to hope for. She'd quit the graduate program that was slowly killing her soul. She'd chosen him. Come back to him. And they'd have the summer to figure out what came next.

Beckett skimmed a hand over her cheek. "It'll all work out okay. It has to."

"Why's that?"

"Because I love you. Nothing else matters more than that."

Stunned pleasure flickered over her features, before those big Bambi eyes went shimmery with unshed tears. "I love you, too. Being with you makes the whole not knowing what comes next less scary."

Without breaking eye contact, he reached out and flipped the lock on the door. "I may not know the next eighty-two steps of what comes next, but I know what comes next right now."

With a little laugh, she looped her arms around his shoulders. "And what's that?"

Backing her toward the table where he'd first tasted her mouth, Beckett set about proving that the answer was unequivocally her.

EPILOGUE

The boathouse had been transformed for the last night of the last camp session of the summer for the sock hop. As they'd prepped, the guys had all bitched that there were too many strings of twinkle lights, but Sarah thought there was no such thing. It was cozy and romantic. All those tiny lights reminded her of private nights at Firefly Falls. She was grateful for the mood lighting that hid the burn of her cheeks at those memories.

All around the room, guests and staff were beginning to take their seats at the round tables lining the perimeter. From her position on the dais, she plugged her laptop up to the waiting projector and pulled up the slide show presentation she'd prepped for the night. Shortly after her return to Camp Firefly Falls, she'd begun taking pictures of the guests and goings on around the facility. It had started out as practice, but when Heather and Michael found out, they'd had her start formally documenting each session, creating a photo slide show of the week that guests could download after their stay.

Beckett stepped up behind her, dropping a kiss to the shoulder bared by her tank top. "Nearly done with set up?"

"Almost." She connected the audio to the waiting speakers and set the presentation to play. It would be background to the rest of the guests arriving, keeping everyone entertained until Heather made her closing night remarks.

Sarah hit play. Once assured the presentation was functioning as intended, she followed Beckett back to the row of staff tables at the far side of the room.

"Glory hallelujah, we're almost through!" Laura did a little shimmy that made her poodle skirt swing. "The *Grease* theme was fun, but I'm ready to get fully back to the twenty-first century."

Beckett rolled his shoulders, which only served to highlight the muscles in his arms beneath the tight black t-shirt. "Tomorrow cannot come soon enough."

Sarah's lips twitched as she tweaked the single gelled curl on his forehead. "Oh, I don't know. Seeing you as a T-Bird has been kind of awesome."

He pulled her in, sliding a hand beneath her pink satin jacket. "That's doing it for you, huh?"

She just grinned and brushed her lips to his.

They took their seats as Heather took her place at the mic. The music faded and the presentation ended on a gorgeous sunset shot Sarah had captured of Lake Waawaatesi.

"Good evening everyone! Let's give a round of applause to our camp photographer, Sarah Meadows." " Heather beamed a smile as everyone clapped.

Sarah offered a little wave.

"If you'd like a copy of these shots, they'll be available for download from the Camp Firefly Falls website. Details will be provided on checkout tomorrow morning. Now, I know you're all eager to get to the dinner and dancing part of this party, so I'll keep this short. This has been an absolutely incredible summer."

It *had* been an amazing summer. Guests would be departing over the course of tomorrow morning, leaving camp purely to the staff for one last week of fun just for them before everything shut down until next season. Sarah found herself a little sad about that. She'd found herself here, and actually learned to *relax*. Mostly. A whole three months had passed, and the world hadn't collapsed just because she didn't know precisely where she was going next. A fact that her twin took great joy in crowing over.

Taryn herself had taken a job with the eccentric Hollywood exec who'd been the cause of all this in the first place as his combination private adventure coordinator and scene scout. She absolutely loved the variability of her job and had been paid so well to do it, she was finally able to divest herself of the last of the stupid debt. The memory of Jax Howarth and all his bullshit could finally be buried for both of them.

Sarah felt really, truly mentally free for the first time in her life. She was head over heels in love with an amazing guy who not only truly understood her, but he'd gone out of his way to save her from herself. Now that she'd had longer than two weeks off from school, she recognized exactly how burnt out she'd been and how desperately she'd needed to get away from academia. This summer had gone a long way toward helping her recover from all that

Courtesy of lodging being included as part of the summer's salary, she'd managed to squirrel away a decent amount of savings. Her apartment had been sublet before she left New York, and all her stuff put into storage. A decision would have to be made about all of that at some point. But right now she was enjoying existing in the present moment.

"It's been an absolute privilege for Michael and me to be a part of your vacation experience. We love this place, and we're blessed to be able to share that love with all of you. We hope you'll come back to see us for another session next year to continue the new legacy of Camp Firefly Falls. Now, please, enjoy the party."

As "Rock Around The Clock" began to pour out of the speakers, staff and guests alike rose and made a beeline for both the dance floor and the buffet set up at the end of the building. Sarah and Beckett stayed put to let the chaos settle.

"I can't believe it's nearly over," she murmured.

He brushed a kiss to her temple. "Just making room for the next thing."

Sarah would've felt better if she knew what that was.

"Beckett? Sarah?"

They looked up to find an older gentleman in

his early fifties standing with his silver shot hair greased back in much the same style as Beckett's.

Sarah smiled. "Hey Trent. How was the hike today?"

"A welcome relief from all the fifties-themed everything. I love my wife, but dear God, a man can only take so much."

Sarah's lips twitched. Trent Cunningham had given his wife this week at camp for an anniversary present because *Grease* was her favorite movie. He hadn't realized exactly how hard-core the theme would be when he agreed to come along. In between all the dance classes, fifties makeovers, and karaoke, he'd ended up spending every day in their neck of the woods, climbing, ziplining, and hiking in the nearby state park. Sarah liked the guy.

"Looking forward to getting home?" Beckett asked.

"Yes and no. Actually, I wanted to talk to you both about something."

Sarah exchanged a look with Beckett. "Have a seat."

Trent made himself at home, sitting across the table. "I had a chat about you with Michael Tully today."

Beckett frowned. "Both of us? Why?"

"Because I wanted to see if his impression of you matched mine. And it does. He gave you both a glowing recommendation."

"Recommendations for what, exactly?" Sarah asked.

Trent smiled. "I'm getting ahead of myself. I'm CEO of TerraVenture Outdoors."

Sarah blinked. "The outdoorwear company?" She owned a pair of their hiking boots.

"We started there, but over the past five years, we've expanded into being the one stop shop for outdoor adventure. Now we're expanding again. Our website caters to outdoorspeople who want to plan outdoor treks around the world. It connects map and planning to gear acquisition, helping make sure all our clients are properly outfitted for their chosen sort of expedition."

"That's impressive," Beckett observed.

"Michael told me about your park service experience, and I've seen Sarah's photography first-hand now. I think the two of you would be a perfect fit as some of our new trail ambassadors."

"That is that, exactly?"

"It would be a sort of travel blogger position. You'd be fully outfitted and sent to effectively review the expeditions we offer, documenting all of it with photo and video and literally showing people what sort of trips they can book through TerraVenture."

Sarah stared at him. "That's not a real job." At his arched eyebrow, she added, "Is it?"

"It's not conventional, that's for sure. But it's a real paying gig. A year-long contract to start, with an option to renew or transition, depending on the growth of that segment of the company."

"What sort of salary are we talking?" Beckett asked.

Trent named a figure that had Sarah wheezing out a breath.

"I know this is a lot, and you don't have to make a decision right now. I can email you both with the particulars, so you can talk it over together."

They gave him their email addresses, then shook his hand.

"Thank you for the opportunity, sir," Sarah said.

"Thank you for keeping me sane in the midst of this 1950s flashback. I look forward to hearing from you."

Neither of them spoke for several moments after he walked away.

"Did that just happen?" she asked.

"Pretty sure it did. He wants to pay us to travel and talk about it. And for you to take photos of it."

"Is there some red flag we aren't seeing? Because this totally sounds too good to be true."

"I mean, we'd obviously have someone review any contracts he sent over, but... my gut says he's legit. I think this is the Universe telling us what's next." Beckett draped an arm over the pack of her chair. "How 'bout it? Are you up for an adventure?"

Sarah sat with the idea, waiting for some sense of panic or anxiety, but all she felt was a deep and steady *yes*. It might not be their forever, but it could be their next right now. And for once, she was okay with that.

Leaning in close, she wrapped her arms around his neck. "I can't think of anyone else I'd rather go on an adventure with more than you."

IT WAS ass o'clock in the morning when they started the drive up to the crest of Mount Wellington. In the passenger seat beside Beckett, Sarah clutched her travel mug of coffee like a lover. More than a year and a half on this adventure and she still wasn't a morning person. Probably never would be. He was okay with that. Her look of profound gratitude and "You are my superhero" when he greeted her with already made coffee would never get old.

They only had a few more days left in Tasmania, and sunrise shots over Hobart from the summit had been high on Sarah's list. They'd attempted this yesterday, but the peak had been shrouded in clouds. Hopefully, today would go better. There was little traffic at this hour as they turned onto the winding road that twisted its way up to the top. Only a few other intrepid souls who had the same idea to see the start of the day from what felt like the top of the world.

At the end of the road, they parked in the lot down from the observation decks, beside a handful of other vehicles. The air was a lot colder at this elevation. Beckett's breath puffed out as he leaned into the backseat to grab a coat. Sarah shrugged into her own, looking a little more alert now that the coffee had been finished.

She snagged her camera bag. "Looks like this morning might go better. I wanna get down to the end of the platform and set up before anybody else shows up to spoil the shot."

There was still some cloud cover and mist swirling around them as they strode past the observation tower and down to one of the lower decks. She paid little attention to the other people, too focused on her task. But Beckett saw the woman hanging back near the observation tower, her blonde hair pulled into a braid, a baseball cap pulled low enough to hide her face. As she spotted him, her smile flashed bright and she shot him a thumbs up.

Right. All was ready for what he had planned this morning.

Despite the cold, his palms felt damp, and he swiped them on his pants as he trotted down the wooden boardwalk steps after Sarah.

The past eighteen months had been incredible. They'd traveled all over the world, exploring outdoor adventures and documenting them. TerraVenture had been so delighted with their work, they'd been offered permanent positions with the company, continuing to do the work they loved. He'd so enjoyed getting to see Sarah bloom, shaking off all the self-imposed rules and restrictions and sense of responsibility. She'd begun making a name for herself in nature photography circles, and Beckett himself had been able to leverage his new platform to push the conservation message that still mattered so much to him from his National Park Service days. Neither of them could have imagined this life when they'd met at Camp Firefly Falls, but Beckett was absolutely certain he didn't want to do this with anyone else. He hoped Sarah felt the same, or this was gonna get awkward really fast.

She already had the tripod out and was selecting the lens she wanted. Not wanting to distract her, he hung back looking up at the stars in the gaps between the clouds. The sky seemed a little lighter now, the endless black giving way to a warmer navy that told him sunrise wasn't too far off. At the camera, Sarah was adjusting settings and muttering to herself. Then she took off the lens cap, stuffing it into the pocket of her puffer jacket.

"Now, we wait."

"So we do. " He reached into the pocket of his own jacket, fingers closing around the small box there.

They lapsed into a comfortable silence. It was such an incredible gift to be with a woman he could be silent with as easily as carrying on a conversation. They simply got each other. They were happy. There was absolutely no reason to expect this to go badly. Still, Beckett was nervous. Asking the woman you loved to spend the rest of her life with you was scary business, even if you were 99.999% positive she was going to say yes.

Shoulder to shoulder they watched the sky continue to lighten, the blues giving way to stunning pinks and oranges. The moment the first rays of the sun burst free of the distant horizon felt spiritual, perfect, broken only by the occasional click of the shutter.

Beckett could feel Sarah's excitement, though she said nothing to break the relative quiet. This was what she'd wanted from this place. These were the money shots.

As the golden orb fully cleared the horizon, he heard the shutter click once. Twice. Three times before she muttered, "Absolutely beautiful."

Knowing this was the moment, Beckett dropped to one knee behind her. "Absolutely."

She straightened and turned, her mouth falling open at the sight of him kneeling on the boards. He was glad he'd waited for her to get the shot he knew she wanted, because in the moment, he wasn't sure she remembered her camera even existed.

"Beckett," she breathed.

"We've been on a hell of an adventure, you and I. At this point I've loved you across most of the continents on this planet. I'm hoping you'll marry me while we knock out the rest and keep building the life we want together. How 'bout it, Sarah? Be my wife?"

The rising sun glinted off the tears in those big Bambi eyes. "Of course it's yes. I wouldn't want to go on any adventure without you."

Grinning, he surged to his feet, arms going around her as his mouth found hers.

Another shutter clicked from somewhere behind them. "Oh, yeah. That's the shot."

Sarah's head jerked up, and she gaped. "Taryn?"

Her sister beamed, lowering the camera in her hands. "Hey, sis. Congratulations."

"What are you *doing* here?"

"Beckett brought me in to document, what with you being busy saying yes and all."

He pulled her even closer. "I thought it was fitting she be a part of this since we would never have even met without her."

She draped her arms around his neck. "That right there is proof that you are absolutely perfect."

"Well, perfect for you, anyway."

"Damn, you two are cute. Does this mean you're going to do a segment on best foreign places to elope?"

But Sarah just waved her sister away and kissed him. Beckett wouldn't have had it any other way.

~

Choose Your Next Romance

I HOPE you enjoyed this trip back to Camp Firefly Falls! I never get tired of grown up summer camp.

If you're looking for more trips away from normal life, check out my Kilted Hearts series about a small Highland village. It begins with *Cowboy in a Kilt,* a true fish out of water tale about a cowboy screwed out of his family inheritance who ends up winning a Scottish barony in a high stakes poker game and ends up having to fulfill a 300 year old marriage pact to keep it! It is, as you might imagine, complicated.

Or maybe you'd like a longer series to sink your teeth into? My Wishful Romance series has twelve books, plus spinoffs! It begins with *To Get Me To You.*

OTHER BOOKS BY KAIT NOLAN

A complete and up-to-date list of all my books can be found at https://kaitnolan.com.

KILTED HEARTS
SMALL TOWN CONTEMPORARY SCOTTISH ROMANCE

- *Jilting The Kilt* (prequel)
- *Cowboy in a Kilt* (Raleigh and Kyla)
- *Grump in a Kilt* (Malcolm and Charlotte)
- *Playboy in a Kilt* (Connor and Sophie)
- *Protector in a Kilt* (Ewan and Isobel)
- *Single Dad in a Kilt* (Hamish and Afton)
- *Kilty Pleasures* (Jason and Skye)

BAD BOY BAKERS
SMALL TOWN MILITARY ROMANCE

- *Rescued By a Bad Boy* (Brax and Mia prequel)
- *Mixed Up With a Marine* (Brax and Mia)
- *Wrapped Up with a Ranger* (Holt and Cayla)
- *Stirred Up by a SEAL* (Jonah and Rachel)
- *Hung Up on the Hacker* (Cash and Hadley)
- *Caught Up with the Captain* (Grey and Rebecca)

RESCUE MY HEART SERIES
SMALL TOWN MILITARY ROMANCE

- *Someone Like You* (Ivy and Harrison)
- *What I Like About You* (Laurel and Sebastian)
- *Bad Case of Loving You* (Paisley and Ty prequel) Included in *Made For Loving You* (Paisley and Ty)

THE MISFIT INN SERIES
SMALL TOWN FAMILY ROMANCE

- *When You Got A Good Thing* (Kennedy and Xander)
- *Til There Was You* (Misty and Denver)
- *Those Sweet Words* (Pru and Flynn)
- *Stay A Little Longer* (Athena and Logan)
- *Bring It On Home* (Maggie and Porter)
- *Come Away with Me* (Moses and Zuri)

MEN OF THE MISFIT INN
SMALL TOWN SOUTHERN ROMANCE

- *Let It Be Me* (Emerson and Caleb)
- *Our Kind of Love* (Abbey and Kyle)
- *Don't You Wanna Stay* (Deanna and Wyatt)
- *Until We Meet Again* (Samantha and Griffin prequel)
- *Come A Little Closer* (Samantha and Griffin)
- *Just Wanted You To Know* (Livia and Declan)
- *A Love Like You* (Juliette and Mick)

WISHFUL ROMANCE SERIES
SMALL TOWN SOUTHERN ROMANCE

- *Once Upon A Coffee* (Avery and Dillon)

- *To Get Me To You* (Cam and Norah)
- *Know Me Well* (Liam and Riley)
- *Be Careful, It's My Heart* (Brody and Tyler)
- *Just For This Moment* (Myles and Piper)
- *Wish I Might* (Reed and Cecily)
- *Turn My World Around* (Tucker and Corinne)
- *Dance Me A Dream* (Jace and Tara)
- *See You Again* (Trey and Sandy)
- *The Christmas Fountain* (Chad and Mary Alice)
- *You Were Meant For Me* (Mitch and Tess)
- *A Lot Like Christmas* (Ryan and Hannah)
- *Dancing Away With My Heart* (Zach and Lexi)

WISHING FOR A HERO SERIES (A WISHFUL SPINOFF SERIES)
SMALL TOWN ROMANTIC SUSPENSE

- *Make You Feel My Love* (Judd and Autumn)
- *Watch Over Me* (Nash and Rowan)
- *Can't Take My Eyes Off You* (Ethan and Miranda)
- *Burn For You* (Sean and Delaney)

MEET CUTE ROMANCE
SMALL TOWN SHORT ROMANCE

- *Once Upon A Snow Day*
- *Once Upon A New Year's Eve*
- *Once Upon An Heirloom*
- *Once Upon A Coffee*
- *Once Upon A Campfire*
- *Once Upon A Rescue*

SUMMER FLING TRILOGY
CONTEMPORARY ROMANCE

- *Second Chance Summer*
- *Summer Camp Secret*
- *The Summer Camp Swap*

ABOUT KAIT

Kait is a Mississippi native, who often swears like a sailor, calls everyone sugar, honey, or darlin', and can wield a bless your heart like a saber or a Snuggie, depending on requirements.

You can find more information on this *USA Today* best selling and RITA ® Award-winning author and her books on her website http://kait nolan.com.

Do you need more small town sass and spark? Sign up for <u>her newsletter</u> to hear about new releases, book deals, and exclusive content!